RAVEN WHISTLE AND STONE

Michael Lewis Owen

Michael is a teacher and writer.

His published writing includes:

GCSE English
1999 Studymate Series

Spell Poems
ZigZag Education English Spelling

Grammar Poems
ZigZag Education English Grammar

Poetry 1380 to 1900 - From Chaucer & Wyatt to Arnold & Hopkins   A Guide for students and teachers - Illustrated
(1st Edition Bracken Press; 3rd Edition Amazon)

Dog at the Window
Dog Poems of Fun and Laughter - Illustrated
(Amazon)

*Carry Your Shoes and Come**
Mindful Poetry (with music) - Illustrated
(Amazon)
Reviewed *'Africa'* April 2024 Issue

*All royalties from this publication are paid directly to Hope House/Tŷ Gobaith children's hospices in England and Wales, to help fund their care for children diagnosed with life-threatening conditions.

Michael lives and works in North Wales.

Acknowledgements

Thank you to my wife Sue, my first editor and best critic, who helped me to iron out many weaknesses in the early drafts of this story, you're simply the best.

I'm grateful to my children James and Mary, who along with their many friends, gave me valuable insights into adolescence so I didn't need to rely on the distant memories of my own!

I'm indebted to James and Lyndsay for their help with the formatting of the text and for their cover design. Thank you also to Craig for help with the *Raven Whistle and Stone* map

I owe much to my three labs, Mima, Maggie-May and Myfanwy, who taught me most of what I know about dogs.

Finally, I need to thank my friend, Ann Tegwen Hughes, for being my expert on all things Welsh, for her enthusiasm and her translation of the sonnet; 'A good dog, a true dog, running home.' I have often glimpsed how lucky the university students under her tutorage must have been, as she has patiently helped me to improve this story, making sure it reads as well as possible for my readers. Diolch yn fawr, Ann

For:

Sharon Duffy 1973 - 1986 (RIP) and for all children facing a challenge like hers.

Key places in: *Raven Whistle and Stone*

CHAPTER 1

Dreams!

As far back as she can remember Sasha Littlejohn has always had vivid dreams, disturbing dreams affecting her conscious mind. Dreams she cannot seem to get out of her head, as if they have a life of their own. Since she's been dating Alex, two dreams are constantly haunting her. They come to her repeatedly in the hours just after midnight, always in the same order. The first appears to have nothing to do with Alex, he is only in the second dream, the frightening one - the nightmare.

The first dream is calming. It empowers her. It moves her deeply with a longing in the very core of her being. It's complicated. There seems to be a lot for her to learn. Each time the dream comes she understands a little bit more. One part that resonates with her is the question that's always asked, 'Who is the Searcher?'

A dapple grey horse, shimmering like starlight, travels towards her. A mysterious lady is riding, serene but strong. Her dark cloak displays a crescent moon and star. Her face is covered but as she approaches silver light showers the ground, falling soft as snow, bringing peace. The sort of peace you feel when everything is ready, presents are wrapped, the table is laid, beds are made for friends who are coming, there's nothing left to do except wait.

Sasha is curious. She wants to catch up with the rider to learn more about her and the beautiful horse. So she begins to trot after the lady. The horse does not seem to be hurrying, just moving smoothly along. At first, she thinks she'll easily catch up with it, yet no matter how fast she goes the distance between them remains the same. She begins to sprint her fastest but cannot keep going and has to rest, panting for breath. Now the distance between them is growing steadily. Sash watches helplessly, knowing she can never overtake the horse and lady.

Suddenly the rider stops her horse, turns to look back at Sasha, her cloak alight with the brightness of stars. Her voice, like the cooing of a pigeon, soft and clear on the air, carries this plaintiff message:

'The Searcher is needed. The time of temptation is here. The test will be terrible. The Keeper, the Finder, the Reader, they all await the Searcher. They are frightened but ready. Where is the Searcher? When will the Searcher come? Who is the Searcher?

Try not to be troubled, deeply I mean, in the pure part of your being. Keep true, accept sorrow with all its hurtfulness. It is the other side of the coin from happiness. Your joy is the cause of your sorrow, you cannot have one without the other. Tears of sadness spring from love, peace flows from both. So grieve when you have cause to be sad but be kind to yourself as well, put a friendly arm over your own shoulder so then you can help another.'

The lady and horse begin to move away. They blend with the darkness becoming lost to sight but Sash hears the rider's last words falling out of the night sky:

'Follow your heart my lovely, follow, follow, follow ...'

The second dream fills her with dread. It comes quickly, bringing a terrifying intensity:

She's cycling, leading Alex through the winding streets of

Clitheroe. It's a place she's never visited but strangely she is the one who knows the way. She twists down past a castle and is aware of Pendle Hill leaning over, high above - an abode of witches.

The road is black. She goes into a left bend where the tarmac's frosted. She worries Alex may be lost but cannot look behind because it's so slippery. She grips the handlebars as the gradient takes the wheels spinning ever faster down the icy road. She knows she cannot brake, the wheels will lock and take her into a skid then she won't be able to steer.

In the distance, moving towards her along the road is something dark and strange. She cannot work out what it is, partly because the wind in her face is freezing, making her eyes water.

There's a humpback bridge ahead. She slows a little as the road flattens and whitens in a thin layer of crisp snow which helps reduce her speed. Now she's below the bridge she can see great icicles pointing like giant fingers at the frozen river underneath.

She can hear a rhythmic trudge, sedate but many footed, approaching the bridge on the far side. There's a terrible rumbling, a grinding of iron on stone, a crushing of ice. What is it? Where's Alex?

The air is arctic making her nostrils twitch. The breeze should smell good but is tainted. There's something on the other side of the bridge … something she never wants to meet … it's coming her way!

She stops to look round for Alex.

He's a speck in the distance. At his side is a hound, a gigantic hound, its coat is dazzling white but its ears burn like lighted coals. She feels relief, 'The Hound of Arawn runs!' she breathes aloud.

Then her attention is drawn forward. The trudge of the many

footed thing is louder. Two plumes of black feathers rise into view, now two more and then two again - six. Attached to the feathers come dark horses with flared nostrils, their eyes gleam with fire.

She is reassured by the glorious animals and relaxes. She puts her right foot down on to the ground and pulls her bike to the edge of the road to let the horses pass. They are pulling a huge carriage. It is covered in black cloth. She wonders what it can be before she realises it's a horse-drawn Victorian hearse.

The bad smell is stronger in the air, foul. Its sour taste shrivels her tongue. The coachman is wearing a black hat, a topper, and a purple cape. He is crouched over the reins looking dead ahead but, as he passes her, he turns towards her to glare with yellow eyes. His thick tail ripples with muscle, smooth and black. It twists to a point. She knows instinctively: he can use it as a spear or a whip, use it at will to hurt as he pleases …

◆ ◆ ◆

Sasha's kid sister Sal, sometimes known as Little Sal is prone to dreams as well. Perhaps it's something in their genes?

Of course everybody dreams but these two girls are professionals. Sash is terribly upset about Sal's illness, it's her real life nightmare, something she has to live with every day. At least with a nightmare you wake up and escape into reality, but every morning Sash remembers on waking: how Sal is so desperately ill.

It's something she's learning to live with, something impossibly hard. One thing she's learnt is she isn't as strong as Sal. Sal's been amazing.

CHAPTER 2

Little Sal is bravely enjoying her last few weeks of school. Everyone knows she will be dead before the end of the summer. Her cancer is in its final stage, eating her alive.

It's May 1970.

Sixteen year old Alex Edwards is stunned at what she's saying. His spine's tingling. His body hairs are going electric, shivering up his back.

Sal's sitting opposite him in the school canteen. She's chirping away in her high pitched voice about her dreams. She's the twelve year old sister of his girlfriend, Sasha, and is telling him how she dreams about the same places nearly every night.

He's listening to her with rising shock.

She's describing her dream world but he knows this place inside out. It's where his mum was born. It's the place where his uncle, aunt and cousins still live! 'Really weird but unmistakable all the same! How can she possibly know all this?' he wonders. He squeezes the inside of his thigh, giving a vicious pinch, to make certain he's awake and this is real.

He looks across at Sal's shaved head, into her greeny-grey eyes. She's explaining, 'I'm back there often in those hills - you and Sash are there too. Last night the sun was shining on the heather. Its light was catching a dead fir with some decayed stumps on either side, a sad but happy sight all in one, you know what I mean? A raven was doing amazing acrobatics. It was above the moor, across the slatey hillside then flying out over the copper-sulphate lakes down in the valley below! You should've seen it!'

'Copper-sulphate Sal! Do you mean they were blue? Did you have double science yesterday?' he laughs trying to hide his feelings.

Sal giggles happily, 'As a matter of fact I did. Do you think it's affected my dreams? Certainly a copper-sulphate lake does sound a bit much, I get that.'

'A bit odd but not as weird as the rest of it,' Alex thinks to himself.

A girl with a bob of black hair sweeps in. Putting her arm around Sal, she kisses the top of her head lightly.

'Hi big sis,' Sal says looking up into Sasha's eyes, blue like those lakes she's been dreaming about.

Alex looks across at the sisters, smiling a greeting to Sash, 'Sal's been telling me about her dreams.'

'Oh yeah, which one? Is it the trendy one with all that sand, sunshine, water and springs and skippy happy clappy?'

'Not today Sash, it's that place in the hills with the lakes, the dead fir and the moor - the one you and Alex are in …'

'Oh I like that happy place more Sal, specially the way you describe it in your dream diary,' Sash interrupts quickly.

'So you keep a dream diary, Sal?'

'Yes but it's secret, so don't let on, will you?'

'Am I going to see it at all?'

Sal glances at Sasha and then looks back at Alex, 'Praps … but I must get going now.' She looks quickly at her watch, 'It takes me ages to get from here to French.' Up she struggles, grabs hold of her walking frame and shuffles off, her pink satchel perched on her back.

Sash sighs.

'You okay?'

'Yeah, but sometimes it gets to me - it's like this void in my head, deathly dark. She's so chirpy and not fwightened at all,' Sasha confides, lapsing through stress into the lisp she's outgrown. 'Just look at her,' she adds glancing across at Sal approaching the door, 'she's so bold, so ill but so strong too - she says she's not going to miss a single day of school.'

'I know. I remember passing her in the corridor at the beginning of term. I had that Monday morning after Christmas feeling, steamy windows running with condensation, ugh wishing I was still in bed! Lines of glum faced kids, teachers, all bumbling along … then there was Sal battling through on her frame, giving me a massive grin as we passed - amazing!'

Sasha nods, flashing him a smile.

'So, tell me more about this dream diary, Sash?'

'Oh she's got this other world she goes to. Sal says when she's there she never wants to come back here. It's a happy place where she can run and climb. She doesn't need her frame at all. She's got a special friend there. She simply adores being with him. Everyone else in her dream's happy and friendly too, they're all full of fun.'

'Do you remember Jess's little brother?' she asks.

'Yeah, of course, Tommo, the boy who died of meningitis.'

Alex looks at Sash intensely and she pauses a moment.

'Well Sal's met him in her dreams and had a great time playing beach skittles with him. Her special friend is friends with

Tommo too, calls him big bro and follows him everywhere.'

'Sounds like heaven.'

Sash smiles bleakly, 'It does - trouble is Sal says she'll soon be there for good which may be okay for her, but we're gonna miss her so much and I don't know how Mum will cope.'

'Yeah, I get that Sash.' Alex reaches over and gives her hand a squeeze. Then a thought strikes him, 'Hey, do you think Sal would let me see her dream diary?'

'I expect so. She likes you a lot and is always chatting about you to me.'

'What about?'

'Just girls' talk,' her cheek dimples. 'Call round for tea, I expect she'll let you take a peek at it.'

'Okay, thanks.'

'Well I've gotta hurry, it's Old Hasty next!'

'Good luck, see ya later then.'

She gets up to go. Spontaneously, he begins singing the number they love, Mungo Jerry's huge hit riding high at Number One about the summer time, when the weather is fine.

This makes Sash laugh. She dances off, weaving her way through the tables and chairs, singing to herself, while he watches her as she sways her hips out through the open doors.

He finishes off his cheese roll, chewing over in his mind how well he knows the stone strewn slope, the dead fir-tree with a decayed stump on each side and the pair of lakes below. He knows them all right - but it's so strange that Sal has been dreaming of that place, when she's never been anywhere near there. How come she's been dreaming of him around Tirion Lakes with Gob the Dog and Sash?

CHAPTER 3

Alex sprawls lazily in bed, Sal's dream diary lies on the bedspread beside him, its furry purple cover blending somewhat with the blue of his room.

He's thinking of his first date with Sash ...

... that warm feeling of holding her close under the old-fashioned lamp of the London street after they'd left the party. He feels again their togetherness as she nestles into him, the sense of belonging. Now he can see the young cop on his beat ... walking slowly towards them ... the sense of peace and goodness lingering as the policeman discreetly turns, walks away so as not to intrude - yes Sash is per-fec-tion.

Smiling, he picks up the diary to read it.

Private!!! You should NOT be reading this without permission!!!

Sand-dunes and Sea - Yippee!

I've been dreaming a lot about this place. I want to remember it all so I'm writing it down, just for me.

The sun shines, those dunes glisten green and warm. I have loads of friends of course and can run, play and swim -Yes, I'm free of pain! Bro is my special friend, he seems to be friends with everyone. He calls everyone Bro you see so that's become his name - cool isn't it. I love Bro ....

Surprise! Surprise!

Imagine the shock I had the other day when Bro was jumping down a sand-dune and Tommo came skipping along by the sea - yeah I mean Tommo! Bro shouted, ' Hiya big bro!' as he does you know.

'Tommo!' I joined in, screaming in joy.

Tommo just came running over - hugged me so hard I thought I would burst with happiness. Bro was laughing.

Then a whole gang arrived and we were all friends and playing - singing and laughing, just great! A warm breeze was blowing from the land. The sunlight on the sea was dancing on the waves, pouring joy on everyone and everything.

Afterwards, Tommo sat with Bro and me.

It was like I'd always been there but Tommo asked, 'Are you living here now?'

That jolted me a bit, I had to think before answering because I was IN MY BED AT HOME!! I stammered, 'N…no … but I come here often when I'm dreaming, don't I Bro?'

Bro smiled. He put his arm over my shoulder, 'You're always dreaming your way here, Sis.'

He made me feel just brill! That's what he's like, see?

We sat for a while, saying nothing, just enjoying the sun on the sea, the warm sand between our toes, feeling our friendship but something else as well. It's hard to put the feeling into words, I suppose. Yeah, that's it PEACE - peace that you could almost touch, if you know what I mean?

Something New Now … Something Really Nice for Meeee!

I so look forward to going to sleep because I know I'll be back by those dunes with my friends.

Well, this last visit was different. It started the same: playing in the sun with our gang and being able to run and climb. Being free from pain! - just happy, being so happy, so myself, so at peace.

Then Bro took my hand and, giving Tommo and the others a wave, he led me - just me - away into the dunes, following the sandy path up and down, away from the sea. REALLY EPIC!!!

We came to a big space where there were blackberries galore. They were juicy, delicious, easy to pick. Yum!

Then we climbed a hill. To our left, was an amazing walled palace! At the front was a pool of water in a massive shell, with a fountain flowing out of the mouth of a mermaid. So pretty there in the middle of the pool. Listen, I can feel it now as I write this - ooh it's so cool I could almost stick my tongue out again to catch some drops! The fountain water fizzled right through me all the way down to my toes, just FAN-TAS-TIC!

Then I noticed that Bro had grown taller. He seemed at least a year or so older as well. Suddenly a spaniel barked nearby. Next, this liver and white dog bounded towards us, his tail wagging, his eyes sparkling. Bro caressed him easily. Then the dog turned to me, in welcome. I loved him at once! I hugged him, ran the tips of my fingers across his silky coat, rested my face against his neck. He had a medal attached to his collar. I read his name, *Arawn*.

'He's our fearless friend,' Bro said by way of introduction.

Warning: No snoopers allowed! Only read on with permission! Private!!

NB
Note Well or Nota Bene (just writing in Latin as Mr. Fitz taught us)

I've decided I'm going to write all my entries in my best English. Everything here's so important, so special - I must record it properly, give it my best respect.

West Window

I've been back to the walled palace many times now. Today Bro led me down miles of corridors with huge doors appearing on either side as we passed. The alabaster floors were cool, smooth on my bare feet and the walls gleamed white and high. (Did you spot the Fitz word there?) I could not see the ceiling, and never can in the palace, because it's layered in a gold light. Above each doorway a silver trumpet popped out as we walked by playing soft, marching music - giving me a spring in my step.

I walked in a daze of pleasure with Bro. All too soon, we reached the end of the corridor. Before us was a slate-black door.

Bro gave a gentle knock. Soon the face of a DRAGON appeared on its left hand side. Out of the dragon's mouth a banner of green and red letters began to flow until the words, *Cymru, West Window* could clearly be seen.

The door clicked, then swung in on its hinges. As we stepped into the room, the smell of heather, pine and the sea reminded me of our Cornish holiday in Bodmin. Close by, I heard the roar of water and the cry of a curlew high above me. My feet had moved from the smooth alabaster of the corridor to knotted oak boards. It was so real.

Light was streaming in from the window at the far end of the room. We approached to look out onto a world of mountains and moorland.

My eyes travelled over that green and purple land. Strangely I seemed to move into the country with them! Suddenly, I noticed Sash and Alex sitting on a slatey hillside above two lakes that were looking up at me with huge, blue eyes! Alex had his arm over Sasha's shoulder because she was weeping. It made me sad to see her upset, my throat felt sore, tears sprang into my eyes.

They were sitting close together.

Higher up the slope among the stones, I saw a single blackened fir tree and the remains of two stumps, on either side with the fir in the middle.

Away to the east a brown kestrel was holding itself above the moor, fluttering and watching but holding still in the breeze. It was like a golden speck in the sky with the sun bright above it.

Then Alex pointed and Sash looked up. High in the sky, three ravens were playing in the wind and air. Their acrobatics were amazing! Sash began to smile, then she was laughing as the birds tumbled their way down over the lakes below, croaking loudly as they went.

I felt happy too, happiness as well as sorrow. It was amazing to see Alex and Sash waving wildly, jumping high. Gob the Dog was bounding around sensing their excitement.

I tried to shout, I waved but they couldn't see me. They couldn't hear me!

This has got me thinking. I know it was a dream but it was so, so real. How come I could see them but they couldn't see me? Or hear my shouts.

I'm not invisible, AM I?

***

Alex feels a shiver run along his spine, a foreshadowing perhaps? He turns the page and comes to a section which is firmly stitched together by a series of small paper clips. On it is written:

Only to be read during the twelve days of Christmas. Or else!

So he turns the clumped pages over, wondering what on earth

they are about, and continues his reading.

The Writing on the Wall

Bro often takes me to West Window. I have learned to love the country there - wild and free - just like me in my dream country.

I have seen a mighty waterfall and the great river far off, looking tiny in the distance. Often Sash, Alex and Gob are there. I love watching them, seeing their happiness together. Alex's dog likes to leap through the bracken, now you see him, now you don't, just like a dolphin. He makes me giggle with pleasure. I love him, of course, he's so cute.

Tonight Bro stopped to point at the wall to the right of the big window. I hadn't (Whoops - proper English remember) I had not noticed it before, which is strange. A beautiful tapestry was hanging there. Along its edges were woven figures of white deer, suns, stars and moons. At the top in scarlet thread I read the words:

Be Fearless and Brave but Forgiving too

The red thread was shimmering on a green background. When I read one line another appeared:

The Hound of Arawn comes
He runs

Be brave
Be fearless
Be free

Always recall
Forgiveness is
The balm of all

Aenlic Angharad

Underneath this writing, a raven, a green eyed raven, suddenly appeared and beside it was stitched the name, BRAN.

Alex closes the diary. He blinks away a tear that has gathered on his eyelash.

Sal's raised more questions.

How does she know the Welsh valley where his mum was born and where his Aunty Enid and Uncle Berwyn still live?

The Hound of Arawn echoes in his memory, bringing back stories from his childhood, tales told around the hearth, tales he loved as a boy, tales of Welsh myths and magic - but Sal can have no knowledge of them, can she?

Alex knows these are strange dreams indeed, 'Really weird,' he thinks 'no wonder Sash said she preferred the dreams of sand-dunes and sea!'

He turns the fluffy book over and opens the diary at the back. He sees some writing there but it's upside down. 'Why's that?' he asks himself.

Curious, he twists it around and begins to read:

The Other Tapestry

Today, when we were leaving West Window, I noticed a second tapestry. It was hanging on the wall on the other side of the room - to the right of the door as you leave.

To my surprise the whole of it was gold thread. I stopped to look but Bro moved as if to carry on out of the room as usual.

Just as I was going to join him, words began to appear in black, spidery writing that made me think of an old hand, an old ink-well and a dip-pen with a feathery quill. I wanted to catch up with Bro but could not move because the tapestry seemed to have a hypnotic hold on me. You know that feeling in a dream when you try to move but can't, well it was a bit like that you know.

The gold thread was brighter than ever but the black writing was wet, cut deep into the cloth:

Beware ... Beware ... Beware the Sleeker!

The Sleeker is abroad,
The sibilant seeker.

Sliding from the Sargasso

His minions roam,
Spying by night
Seeking
But out of sight.

Suddenly, from nowhere, even though I was completely alone, an unctuous voice was telling me I had a CHOICE.

I could choose something much greater ... *IF I LIKED* ... it purred.

I began to see myself as an older girl. I was wearing a wedding dress. Sash and Mum were with me. We were happy. My hair had grown back; it was styled, neat, pretty under my veil.

I started looking around - puzzled. Where was Alex? He should have been with Sash, why wasn't he there?

The persuasive voice was telling me I could have all this *and much more if* ... it was simpering, oily, trying to get me to agree.

'No, I do not choose it ; I reject it!' I answered emphatically.

Irritated, I found myself having to explain how Bro was my special friend, that I chose to stay with him always ...

While I was speaking I felt a gentle touch of my hand and looked down to see Bro's dog, Arawn, licking my fingers. This strengthened me, making me BRAVE. Strangely, as he licked my hand, the writing was erased and soon all I could see was the gold thread of the tapestry.

I knew somehow that I HAD MADE A CHOICE, an important decision to STAY HERE WITH BRO, like he wanted.

Then I was in the corridor, striding with him and Arawn making out that nothing had happened. We were on our way, heading towards the main door, going on out to the fountain, to the dunes, to the open sea beyond.
Totally Green !!!

I thought nothing in *Cymru, West Window* could surprise me by now as I know it inside out .... How wrong was I?

In my dream last night, I was standing with Bro looking out at the moor. A herd of ponies was grazing peacefully, mares and foals together. I watched a cute colt, his white coat sparkling as he rolled over in the rushes, enjoying a good scratch, having a mud bath. When he clambered to his feet, rusty stripes of peat were scored onto his back. He was soaking! He gave a good shake, sending spray all over his dam - it was funny and made me laugh.

Suddenly there was a rumbling sound. I could feel a vibration running up from my hands. I looked down at them, resting on the wooden windowsill. Strangely the sill was opening, literally sliding away.

Amazed, I looked at what was there in the gap. It was as if I was holding the thing. It was completely GREEN! I could see it really clearly. I knew at once it was magical. The weave of the cloth was so amazing only a human spider could have made it. Just awesome!! All the time it was changing colour, continuously changing, always green but a changing green. I was seeing every kind of green: dark pine, soft willow, pale olive, shiny holly, … the colours were shimmering, rising from it in amazing numbers! Just imagine that, can you? Magic!!

I turned to look up at Bro.

'It's the girdle of Gawain,' Bro said, 'as brave and fair as can be.'

'Who's he?' I asked.

'A good person,' he answered, ' a very good one.'

What did this girdle of Gawain mean with its shimmering greens; its tiny, strong weave - '… fair as can be …?'

'What's a girdle for?' I asked Bro.

'It's a belt or sash but this one was a special gift as well,' he answered. 'Be wary of gifts, Sal, specially if you don't really know the giver.'

'Understood Bro,' and as I replied the sill closed. The cloth was hidden again but now I knew it was there - a secret thing but very important.

We looked out of the window to see the ponies trotting up out of the rushes, running with purpose, almost marching in tight formation as they moved away following the colt and his dam over the heather. Where were they going?

Alex closes the diary.

Sal's finished with a question … there's this massive question mark in his mind. He'd read the diary hoping for answers but it's settled nothing - he realises Sal knows so many details, that she's even seen the wild ponies. The ones he used to love watching in the mountains above his home. It's just astonishing.

Then, as he puts the diary back in its place, a memory tumbles through a door in his mind. It is from a while ago …a time when he'd been helping his Uncle Berwyn's friend, Aled Thomas.

They'd been moving some books into a bookcase when he'd stopped to look at one. It'd caught his eye because its cover was lime green but in its centre was a drawing, just black and white. This showed a pretty woman standing over a man who was lying in bed. He seemed to be sleeping but she was tickling his beard with her index finger. It had made him wonder what would happen when the sleeper awoke. Curious, he'd flipped the paperback open but the writing inside was not a language he could read, 'What's this book?'

'Gawain and the Green Knight,' Aled had answered, 'it's an old work written somewhere just north of here, you'll not recognise many words but it is early English.'

Alex shuts his eyes, thinking hard, knowing there's more … finding his way in the dark like a blind man, he reaches out with his hands. There's nothing to touch or hold, just air but he knows there's something more … if he could only remember it.

CHAPTER 4

Brave to the end, Sal has planned every detail of her funeral by herself.

The church is packed. Alex is feeling tense; his dark suit, crisp, unfamiliar. His shirt white with newness. He doesn't normally go to church except when he's with the family in Wales. It's weird to have Gobaith with him here, the strangeness adds to his general unease but Gob's presence is always also a comfort.

The words of the hymn are rising and falling:

... Bless us, dear Lord
And bless the friends we cherish

Alex knows that when the hymn's over, he is next. Gob's lead is clenched in his right hand. The dog beside him is calm, such a contrast to the stress in his own head.

Sal has asked Alex to read the short speech she's written because she won't be there to do it herself. She'd insisted Gob the Dog must come to her funeral as well. While Alex is doing his reading she's arranged for Gob to sit on the top step, facing her coffin and the congregation.

In her final months, Alex has always taken Gobaith to Sal's bedroom. They've become the closest of friends, so much so Sal demanded a photo of Gob be placed on her coffin next to the single, white lily.

Now, Alex looks up at the wicker coffin - it seems so small. There on its lid, the photo and lily. At the front of the church are Sash,

Sal's Mum, Gloria, and Gloria's twin sister. 'Poor Sash, she lost her dad in that cycling accident and now her kid sister, Sal, has gone too,' he thinks and then swallows trying to clear his throat.

The hymn ends. Silence fills the church. He steps out of his pew and Gob follows. He stops at the coffin for a moment to place his left hand on the lid. It is a touch for Sal, a touch for their friendship and times together - good times.

Then he and Gob are up the steps.
He makes Gob sit, ensuring it's just as Sal planned. The faithful friend sits upright: looking down on Sal's coffin and over the congregation; alert, respectful, still.

Alex moves to the lectern. The paper with Sal's speech is there, written in her handwriting, waiting for him. He looks down at Sasha - glimpsing her red-rimmed eyes. He is determined to do this as well as he can for Sal and for Sash. He tries to calm himself, knowing he must not read her words too quickly, looks up and begins:

"Thank you for coming to my funeral.

I've asked Alex to let Gob the Dog sit and face you. Have you ever seen a dog in church before?

I've known I was dying for a while but I'm not afraid ... well not anymore. That's because I've seen where I'm going - after I die I mean. It's a lovely place, I can tell you. Also, I've seen Gob there. It's strange I know but he's in both places. He is an amazing dog, truly amazing.

Really I want to tell you just one thing - animals are more important than we think. Believe me, they are vital. The smallest insect, the tiniest bird and the slenderest fish all hold the key to the goodness of our Earth - so listen everyone, you must look after them. They are more precious than anything. I hope you can see that they are. They really are, you know?

Look at Gob. Look at his innocence. Can you see he's perfect? Can you see his courage? Can you see his other self?

I expect you can't, but I can and I'm seeing him, all of him, now as Alex reads my words to you."

Alex folds the paper as he steps over to the waiting cassette player. He presses the play button firmly to allow Sal's voice to start:

"Thank you, Alex, and to everyone who's here as well."

No-one is more surprised than Gob. He stands up quickly, pricks his ears turning his head attentively to one side and looks for her. Alex motions for him to sit, which he does, hanging on Sal's every word like everybody else in the building.

"I'm going to finish by singing you a short song I've composed." She giggles for a moment, a happy sound in the listening church. "I've cheated a bit really because I used the 'Ash Grove' tune we so loved in the Guides. It's called: 'Watch over our World,' I hope you like it.

The clean air how graceful, how plainly 'tis speaking,
The pure wind is calling ... is talking to me:
'No more let pollution its bad way of breathing
Spoil our land, our country so green and so free.'
The friends from my days here again are before me
Each step brings a loved one as freely I roam.
Soft whispers I'm calling to all who can hear me:
'Care for our Earth mother, our dear precious home.'"

As the singing comes to an end, a collective sigh shudders through the church.

Then Sal's voice is heard, she's speaking from the tape recorder, "I want to share one more thing with you - my body's just like a leaf floating in the wind but there's something huge out here.

It's overpowering, happy, so alive too. I can just let my body float away and belong to something bigger along with all plants, animals, even rocks and earth. Life with all its difficulties is a gift, it's playful, fun and can never be destroyed. Do you get that? Life is vital, real and FOREVER."

◆ ◆ ◆

The rest of the day is a blur of sorrow, greetings and pleasantries with the many, many friends and family who are there. Gob is everyone's friend being stroked and patted again, and again and again.

Eventually they are slumped on the sofa in Sash's lounge and her Mum brings in more mugs of tea. She begins to talk in that fluent, hurried manner of hers, 'The night before she died Sal began to reel off her whole life like she was reporting for a film. She talked a lot about the two of you and about Gobaith, as she likes to call Gob, and about Wales and the mountains, which is strange really because she's never ever been there you know.'

'Sal's right, his name is Gobaith,' Alex responds, 'but I've shortened it to Gob - it's easier to say. Then everyone started calling him Gob the Dog and he answers to that as well so you see he's a dog of many names now.'

Sash has heard all this before but is trying to look interested for Alex's sake.

'Oh, I see,' Gloria says smiling. 'Do you know that when Sal's body was ready to leave the house …?' she breaks off looking at Alex,

Alex doesn't know and shakes his head.

'Well, the doorbell rings three times so I rush down, thinking that it'll be the undertakers, and I open the door and there's nobody there - I look out of the door, up and down the street but there's nobody in sight.' Then Gloria sounds agitated as she asks,

'Who could have been ringing for Sal like that? Might it have been a spirit? Or Sal herself?'

'Yeah it was weally weird,' Sash mutters but so stressed he hardly hears.

'Now Alex you will look after Sash for me won't you while she's in Wales - the break will be good for her I know,' she adds wearily glancing through the open doorway to the pile of plates dumped in the sink. 'And Gob's going with you of course,' Gloria continues, 'wasn't he good today? Everyone's favourite - and so good in the church and playing his part just as our Sal wanted,' she ends breathlessly, dabbing the tears on her cheeks with a handkerchief.

Alex is overcome. He feels an urgent desire to comfort her. He asks gently, 'Did Sal ever tell you what Gobaith is in English?'

'No, Alex, no I don't remember,' Gloria answers, blinking her eyes to clear them. 'Tell me would you? I'd like to know.'

'Hope, Gloria, Gobaith is Welsh for hope.'

CHAPTER 5

'Snap! Beat you again, hee-hee-hee!' Sash teases as she scoops in the last of the cards.

'Ssh you'll wake Gobaith.'

'No I won't he's awake already, his head's on my lap!'

Alex reaches down below the table and finds Gob's head and Sash's knee.

The train is rocking from side to side as it gathers speed on its long journey to Holyhead and the Anglesey coast.

Sash leans her head on his shoulder and they sway with the rhythm of the train. It is late July - the summer holidays stretch before them, a golden track of days reaching into a future they cannot see.

The train plunges into a tunnel. To his surprise Alex finds himself in darkness. He can feel the urgent rhythm of the swaying train and Sash's head is hard and heavy on his arm. 'The driver's going for it, must be making up for lost time,' he thinks and swallows to clear his ears. An eerie, unnatural shrieking fills his head. The train enters a pocket of bad air; his nostrils sense skunk. Then he is whirling, dizzy ... close to blacking out.

Don't play; go away. Don't play with us, a voice sneers. *We'll break you boy. We'll take you to break you, break you like a twig - snap!*

'What's going on?' His fear is rising. He's shivering!

Do not come to Wales. Do not come to Wales. Do not come. Stay away. We will be there waiting. Waiting to break you. Understand?

He feels cold. There's a weight on his arm pulling him down.

Go back ... back... ba...ck! echoes away down the tunnel.

The train pops into the open and he blinks in the bright sunshine.

'You okay?' Sash asks. 'You were shaking your head in the tunnel and your eyes were clenched shut.'

'Yeah, I'm fine - my ears popped a bit, that's all. Did yours, Sash?'

'They did but I just gave a bit of a swallow and they cleared.'

'How do you bite a swallow?'

'I'll show you,' she smirks, turning her mouth against his arm to nip it.

'Ow!' he barely stifles his surprise,

Sash looks up laughing, 'That's how!'

Much of Gloria's packed lunch is shared with Gob. He does not believe in waste, gratefully gobbling all the crusts, cheese rind and smokey bacon crisps that come his way. Before they know it they are on Chester station to change trains for Wales and the west.

Sash loves the names that are called out by the announcer, a string of quaint sounding places where the train is stopping on its way to Holyhead: **'Prestatyn, Rhyl, Colwyn Bay, Llandudno Junction, Llanfairfechan, Bangor, Rhosneigr and Holyhead.'**

'Then it's the ferry for Dublin,' she jokes.

While the train rattles its way into North Wales, Alex and Sash talk excitedly about the Carneddau, the mountains of Eryri and Yr Wyddfa the renowned Snowdon, a magnet for climbers.

Alex tickles Gobaith's ears, 'Well my old friend, how does it feel to be back in the land of your birth?'

Gob gives him a look and licks his hand.

Little does he know that in a matter of hours he will be back before the stonemason, Berwyn Davies. It was Berwyn who bred Gobaith and gave him to Alex five years ago, when the boy had been devastated by the divorce of his parents.

Soon they are on Llandudno Junction station and making their way to the exit.

A lively redhead - all freckles, smiles and blue eyes - is waving happily. Alex rushes over to hug his aunt, 'This is Sash and I think you'll remember Gobaith?'

Beside Enid is her daughter, Nonnie, she's come to meet their train too. 'Hiya,' she exclaims happily, 'croeso i Gymru, welcome to Wales!'

It's been a long journey. Alex and Sash make themselves comfy in the back of the Ford Escort as it hurries along the A470. The sun is low in the sky and the tide is in, so the Conwy Estuary is gleaming with a full load of river and salt water.

Across and behind, Sash glimpses the railway bridge and the towers of Conwy Castle rising high beyond it. Now the car is crossing the bridge at Tal-y-Cafn and then winding its way up from the mighty river, on and up to the Afon Gyffin at Bont.

As they go, Alex can see the tops of the tallest oaks, golden in the setting sun, at Tirion Mawr. His Uncle Berwyn lives there with his dogs. Alex knows that Rhian, Berwyn's cousin and life-long friend, will be in her cottage beside the big house. He looks forward to seeing them both again and introducing Sash.

Then the car turns left over the bridge and up the hill. They climb steeply and rattle and bump their way along the rough road running through the yard of Fferm Carreg Arw. The crazy sheepdog there charges the car's tyres barking furiously but is soon left behind, standing on the track growling. With a sweep and turn the car rolls like a big-dipper before drawing to a halt in the spacious courtyard of Gorswen.

CHAPTER 6

Some sixty miles as the crow flies to the south and west of Gorswen, Michael George is in his university rooms. The hated presence is with him, living in his guts - twisting his stomach. The enemy uncoils; terror freezes him. He knows the Sleeker is stirring, the cruel tormentor riding his mind, cruel, cold, hard as steel. Like a dumb beast of burden, he can only submit. He cannot resist. He cannot escape.

It had been so different just two years ago. He had been enjoying his studies and basking in the reflected glory of Charles, Prince of Wales, living and studying in Aberystwyth, a fellow student. Then Armstrong walked on the moon! A wonderful time to be an undergraduate here on the West Wales Coast - really exciting days.

Oh, if only he had never discovered that manuscript! Beware of strange gifts ... beware of getting something for nothing ... beware of false promises.

It had happened when he was preparing an essay on Celtic crosses for his archaeology tutor. He had been thrilled to find the parchment pushed into the dust jacket of an old reference book. Foolishly dabbling in what he did not understand, this rich son of a shipping magnate had been tempted, then snared.

It had begun with him reading some ancient curses. These caught his curiosity. Hooked, he began to repeat them aloud in his room after dark. Disaster followed, an unctuous voice offering him knowledge, power and more ... In a rash moment he chose to agree ... then it had entered and gripped like a leech.

Now it's always there swelling ... controlling at will ... ruling with darkness.

Suddenly, he writhes feeling the enslaver's power, exerting its evil energy like a smoking volcano inside him so he can barely breathe.

You have carried out my instructions? Brutus - that spaniel dog- the necessary arrangements are made?

'The dog dies tonight.'

That boy, Alex, has dared to come. You are to be close to Gorswen, lurking nearby, go at once. The Hound of Arawn dies tonight; I have to be sure. I must possess the collar. I must seize the whistle - the stone is secured. I have urgent tasks, you are to go now, immediately. I suspect Brutus is the cursed hound; I do not know for sure ... that uncertainty torments... this enrages me!

Black steam swirls around the student, a furious pounding surges in his ears, the stench is unbearable. Sulphur stings his nostrils making him wretch. Cupping his hands over his mouth he gasps, 'I will get ready.'

You will.

Sixty miles or so to the north in Tirion Cottage, Rhian is turning the pages of an old scrapbook. The radio plays choral music, filling the room with soothing voices while her tabby cat licks it paws in front of the flickering fire. A cutting from the *County Times,* yellow with age, catches Rhian's attention.

My Pup

I've named my pup Sirius
Which rhymes with words like serious
That I find quite hilarious!

The dog star high in the sky
Stares down at you and I
Sirius its name - I don't know why.

So my pup's Sirius too
When he's a star I'll show him you.

Above the writing is a photo and the caption reads:
Alex Edwards (11) with his pup.

'Not named Sirius after all but Gobaith and now shortened to Gob - why did he change the name?' she wonders.

Outside the July night is starlit, a sliver of moon lies on its back. Shadows enter the grounds of Tirion Mawr. They do not come through the gates; they keep well clear of the beam of yellow light shining through a chink of Rhian's curtains.

They have slipped across the river, Afon Gyffin, flowing down towards Conwy in the valley below the house. They have climbed up to the house in the dark. They move stealthily in single file.

One of them carries a small bag.

Flitting across the lawn like bats, they are soon creeping round the edge of the orchard. Now they glide round the side of the house reaching the lane at the back. Turning left, they follow the track, passing a tumbledown shed on their right as they climb.

They reach a fenced enclosure part of which is roofed - Berwyn's kennels.

Noses push through the bars to lick their hands in welcome and take the offered biscuits; a torch winks over collars searching the metal discs for the name Brutus - got it! Tails wag; poisoned meat is delivered. The dog gulps it down innocently, an unexpected gift from kind strangers.

Mission accomplished - the shadows back off, two dark shapes sliding their way down past the house to the darkness below.

Stillness reigns amongst the stars. The sliver of moon lies motionless above, while Brutus curls up in pain, silent within his kennel, dying in agony on this summer night.

'The noblest Roman of them all' as Berwyn calls him, lies nose to tail hurting inside. For a moment, the mountain air shivers through the leaves of the big trees. Then stillness returns.

As the shadows creep away from the house, noiseless in their wickedness - the yellow light upstairs in Rhian's bedroom clicks off.

CHAPTER 7

Sasha has settled in happily at Gorswen where she and Nonnie have become firm friends. This morning Sash is sitting above two lakes which reflect the blue of the sky. Gob's sniffing away in the bracken. Alex is beside her, the warmth of his shoulder meeting hers.

From nowhere thoughts of Sal fill her mind, a wave of sadness engulfing her.

Alex, sensing her new mood, puts his arm around her shoulder, squeezing it gently.

She leans into him and sobs, 'It's missing Sal.'

'I understand, I miss her too and I'm not her sister.'

She leans further into him, allowing the comforting drum of his heart to soothe her sadness.

Croaking! It's high in the sky, just above them; a raven wheeling and cavorting on the warm breeze. A second joins it then a third.

Alex sees them and points.

Sash begins to smile, next she's laughing as the great birds play on the breeze. In a flash she's exclaiming, 'Little Sal's watching us! This is in her diary. She sees us here and the ravens! Don't you remember it's exactly what she described?' Excitedly she jumps to her feet, waving frantically not at the birds but into the space above.

Alex jumps up as well waving wildly while Gobaith bounds out of the bracken dancing between them.

The ravens swing down over the lakes and away.

To the east, above the moor, hovers a kestrel. Below it on the stone strewn hillside is a dead fir tree and two decayed wooden stumps. Sash sits quietly brooding.

Alex ruffles Gob's neck behind the ear.

Sash holds her head steady. She clears her mind to recall Sal's diary - it's all so strange! 'What on earth's happening?' The question settles in her mind, her sister's presence close beside it. As if on cue, a feather flutters out of the sky and she catches hold of it, shiny and black, a raven's feather. She pockets it.

'Well if we don't get going we'll be last for lunch with Dr Achebe and Gavin will have scoffed most of it,' Alex says standing up.

'I love the way Gavin calls you the Alex-adding-machine! He's good fun isn't he?'

'Yeah, for a little squirt he's okay.'

Soon they have crossed the Gyffin on a footbridge and are climbing up into the village. Salinas Cottage, above the road, overlooks most of the other houses. It's next to the rectory and small chapel. The sky-blue front door catches the eye with its cat's head knocker but there is no need for them to knock because the door is thrown open and Dr Achebe booms out, 'Gee buddy, is it good to see ya!'

Alex grins and begins to introduce Sash, 'This is Sash Dr Ach ...'

'Hey, call me Jack! Great to meet ya Sash, come on in an' join the others.' His dark face creases into a huge grin and he brushes his hand over the white coils of curly hair on his head.

Nonnie is sitting with Jack's ginger cat, Felix, nestled on her lap. She smiles across at Sash.

Gavin is looking at a photograph of an old stone hanging on the wall. 'Hey Alex, you know that ancient stone face, the one Jack found in the river here?'

'Yeah.'

'Well, it's been stolen. Taken from his cabinet a couple of weeks' ago - no break in, nothing else taken, just the stone.'

'That's odd, who'd do that?' Alex asks, looking at Jack.

All they see are the whites of his eyes as Jack leans back and sighs, 'Just doesn't figure, doesn't figure one bit.' Then he changes the subject, 'Hey bud, have you seen your Uncle Berwyn?'

'Yeah, Sash and I, and Gobaith of course, went straight to Tirion Mawr on Tuesday - he was in a bad way you see, some devil's poisoned his dog, Brutus.'

'Gee I'm mighty sorry to hear that,' Jack leans his head back and looks at the ceiling. 'Berwyn was my first buddy when I moved to this place an' still is.'

Alex nods. 'I'm seeing him tomorrow morning before he goes to check on some slate he's buying.'

'Give him my best bud. Tell him I'm grievin',' Jack says, shaking his head as he goes to open the French doors.

Soon they are out in the back garden, enjoying the spread Jack has put on, finishing with his home baked Maryland cookies. Alex, munching away, says, 'Hey Jack, will you tell Sash how you found the stone? Weirdly she's interested in archaeology,' he teases.

Jack turns to Sash, 'I'm kind of mortal proud of finding it, even if it's been taken now.'

Sash nods intently, 'I get that. My dad used to call me Nosey

Parker Sash or sometimes Snoopy Sasha because I was always looking for fossils, eager to explore iron age forts and things like that,' she says with a laugh.

'You don't say so,' Jack says evidently pleased to meet someone interested in his own hobby. He draws closer to her, deciding to share a bit of his past. 'My people were freed from slavery way back and it's a long journey that's taken me here. I pulled out of the USA just after they killed JFK - just couldn't live in that country after that.' He pauses and shakes his head sadly. 'Most American folk are just great an' JFK was into civil rights, hell of a good president. I figured that if the president wasn't safe, who was?'

'Well a few years back, on a day in June, I was strolling in the sunshine down by the "ol man river" as I call the Gyffin here. As I come to cross the bridge I feel this arm across my shoulder. It pulls me gently an' firmly to the side of the bridge an' it's like I can hear my people singing about their freedom in Africa across the mighty ocean. Gee, did it make me feel good! My people, my ancestors had hold of me an' were getting me to look in the rolling river waters - I hear merriness an' laughter an' then, clear an' awesome - a girl singing her heart out.' He stops for a moment before adding, ' It's so lovely just to recall that singing, ya know.'

Sash is gripped by his account. The others have also come closer to listen. They know the story but don't want to miss a word of it.

'An' it's even lovelier to recall what happened next. Gee, the whole river fills with bubbles, exploding all over the show an' through them I see a truly exquisite face: polished like silver, pure an' gentle like I've never seen before or since.' He pauses in rapture.

Gob sits up. He turns his eyes on Jack as if to ask what happens next.

'Well 'ol man river' rolls on an' carries off that rare vision: bubbles, singing an' beautiful lady. I stand there, just staring at the water an' that's when I see it man - a stone face staring back at me from the river bed!'

A loud knocking at the front door calls Jack away. He goes back into the house, they all follow.

It's Aled Thomas, the rector, Jack's neighbour and friend.

Sash warms to the big man with black, bushy eyebrows at once. He seems to know Alex well and is energetic in his greeting. 'It's good to see you again Alex boyo!'

'Rev Thomas it's great to see you too! Jack has just been telling Sash about the stone face he found in the Gyffin. She's keen on archaeology, fossils and exploring ancient sites.'

'Very sensible young lady, I can see, pleased to meet you I'm sure. The stone was quite a find. Fancy Jack coming all the way from California to pick that stone face out of the river - right under our noses too, eh Jack?'

Jack is laughing, his lined face crinkled with merriment. 'Hey bud, you can tell Sash about your Professor Rees and his cronies an' all.'

'Yes I will. Listen ,Tom-the-Doc Brooks, at Swansea put me in touch with Ifor Rees and he was here in a flash. Very interested indeed - examined the stone closely. Then he told us, much to our surprise mind you, it was not the face of a Celtic river god.'

'What was it then?' Sash asks.

'The great man is of the opinion that it is a likeness of The Aenlic Angharad.'

Sasha feels the breath go out of her. It's a name from Little Sal's dream diary, a flash of light from beyond the grave.

'Sash, the others here will know all about *The Mabinogion,* an old collection of Welsh legends. They were passed on by word of mouth from one generation to another down from the mists of history. The tales are as well known to us in Wales as the legend of Arthur is to the Brits.' He breaks off laughing loudly at himself, 'What am I saying, now? *The Mabinogion* has stories connected with Arthur and his knights in the collection of course!'

Sasha looks momentarily at Alex, he's trying to tell her something.

'Now I'm sure you'll all remember the tale of Pwyll, Lord of Dyfed, don't you?' Aled asks, looking at the others.

'Sure do,' Gavin pipes in. 'I love the description of King Arawn's hounds, white fur gleaming and crimson ears glowing.'

'Arawn?' Sash asks looking in amazement at Alex.

Aled Thomas leans forward excitedly, 'Yes indeed Gavin. You are right, fair play. Now let me tell you that King Arawn and Aenlic Angharad were brother and sister. They go back to a legend that is older than "The Mabinogion" itself, "The White Book of Rhydderch."'

Suddenly, Felix leaps to his feet and bounds lightly out of the French doors. Jack watches him go and then shrugs his shoulders as if to say that cats are a law unto themselves.

Aled Thomas looks back at them, 'Ifor Rees says only fragments of the legend are known. Aenlic Angharad was good beyond compare, renowned for her kindness and purity. Her singing voice, it is said, was one of enchantment itself. She and her brother, King Arawn, flourished in the Otherworld Kingdom reputed to stretch from the Menai in the North to the Dyfi in the south and to the Wye in the east. We know that the kingdom flourishes as I said and is known as The Kingdom of Friends. Then there is no further record except for a broken piece of writing, a remnant of a letter, believed to be written by their chamberlain. Jack, you've got a copy of it here, haven't you?'

'Can we see it?' Gavin asks eagerly.

Jack saunters across the room to a high bookcase in the corner. He reaches for a battered biscuit tin and hands it to Gavin, 'Here bud, take a read, it's kept in this cookie tin.'

Gavin places the tin on the low coffee table, opening it while the others draw round him. He begins to read in an awed voice:

'Today Lord Gwilym and the Mountain Marchers left for the West. There, the threat is worse... the boast from the coast ... evil is the sound ...

... Athelstane, most glorious of warriors, with the Mighty Watchers - thirty their number - together they guard Aenlic Angharad ...'

As he scans down to the bottom of the page his voice intones wretchedly:

'... we are sore ... oppressed.'

He turns the paper over and continues now in a barely audible whisper:

'The trouble it cometh ... away in the West ... Gwilym and the valiant Mountain Marchers ... not a word.

The sound, the terrible noise, the din so dreadful ... Northern Borderlands ... Oh! Oh! Oh!

Doom, our doom approacheth ... Athelstane's Bane and doom ... doom ... doom.'

Gavin stops for a moment, then continues in hushed tones:

'Lost, oh utterly lost, the Aenlic Angharad from her tower she sees .... Oh! Oh! Oh! ... noise so dire ...

They come ... they come upon us from all sides ...'

As Gavin begins to read the final fragment a Welsh lilt enters his voice that lifts their subdued spirits:

'Angharad, she sings, her golden voice rings;
Hark to the harp, oh listen ...
A hound of Arawn comes, he runs.

Lost but saved we are
Guard the stone
Guard! Guard! Guard!

The last hound of Arawn
Here he comes
The Hound of Arawn runs.'

CHAPTER 8

How Sasha wishes she'd packed Sal's dream diary! She remembers seeing the names Arawn and Aenlic Angharad written in its pages - 'Far-out, just downright peculiar,' she mutters to herself. There's so much she wants to ask Alex, as the four of them walk the road back to Gorswen but she knows now is not the time. Fferm Carreg Arw comes into view, it's an untidy farmhouse just below the road, a mess of a place.

A young man's blocking their way. Tall, broad, confident, he stands like he owns the world. The sun's high in the sky behind him making her squint as she looks at him, and look she must. Even at first glance his masculinity unnerves her. He holds her eye, dominant, like a tiger, with his fierce nose pointing down at them. He doesn't smile at the approaching group, but his dark eyes scan them all, one after another, before picking on Nonnie.

Sash feels Nonnie tense up beside her.

Nonnie's heart is racing.

Gareth Vaughan stares hard at Nonnie, his eyes sparkling, 'There's a twmpath Saturday. You coming, cariad?'

Caught unawares by his directness, Nonnie blushes before looking away.

He stands pleased with the effect of his words, allowing himself a slow smile of triumph, revealing his teeth, white - strong like the rest of him, perfect but for the chipped front tooth with its jagged edge.

She's saved by Sash, who's noticed the state of the sheepdog, standing at his heel shivering. The baler twine, roughly coiled round its neck, is to Sash like a flag of ill treatment. The look of the animal makes her angry. Its coat, congealed with mud, barely concealing the thinness of its body, is the final straw. 'Is that your dog?' she spits crossly.

Gareth, seeming to see her for the first time, gives her a long look making her feel like he's undressing her. 'Sheepdog,' he corrects.

'You shouldn't tie him in twine. He looks like he could do with a wash. He's terribly thin, are you feeding him enough?'

'If it isn't Miss Hoity-toity on a visit to the countryside telling me how to manage my sheepdog! Rich I'd say, when she can't even tell the difference between a dog and a bitch. Do you see?'

Now it's her turn to blush. She feels the warm flush of blood in her cheeks, but it doesn't show like Nonnie's.

He's standing there, glaring directly at her, arrogant.

She feels her anger rise. Her eyes blaze back at him, 'How dare he look at her in that way!'

Gareth waits, staring hard into her face as if to say, 'Go on then, if you dare.' Then with a shrug of his shoulders he's away strutting off to the barn, clicking his fingers sharply, 'Come along now Meg or shall I call you Mot to please Miss Hoity?' he asks tauntingly. 'Hey Hugh,' he calls into the barn, ' Miss Hoity here thinks Meg's a dog!'

Sash glimpses a second man inside the barn.

Their mirthless laughter is loud, almost a shout as they make out she's just a, 'Stupid bitch!'

'Come on Sash, don't pay attention to them,' Nonnie says, taking her arm to pull her along the road to Gorswen.

Alex comes up beside her, 'Yeah Sash, we don't give the Vaughans the time of day, do we Gav?'

'Course we don't. Never waste a heartbeat on Rough Stone Farm; they're not worth the bother. Come on Gobaith! Let's run!' Gav shouts hurrying off down the road to his home.

After tea they spend the evening playing a funny acting game which the Lewis family call 'The Manner of the Word.' The funniest moment is when Enid is out of the room and they choose the word 'doggedly.' When she re-enters, they are on all fours, sniffing around, much to Gob's alarm. It takes her ages to guess but she finally gets it when Gav begins barking like the poor dog down the road.

Before turning in for the night, Sash and Alex take Gobaith for an airing. The sky is clear so stars are beginning to show. They stroll a short way from the house towards a wooden gate. The view from there is across the woods, down to the river, then away west to the sea, where the lights of Conwy can be seen in the growing darkness.

They're arm in arm. Sash pulls Alex round to look up into his eyes, 'I wish we'd brought Sal's diary with us. She always said she dreamt of us here in this very place and …'

'Yeah. I remember thinking it was uncanny how she knew my Welsh home in her dreams. I remember wondering about the dog, the fearless friend, Arawn, as well. You're right, Sash, we should have brought it with us.'

'Don't you remember seeing Aenlic Angharad in her diary too?'

'Yeah, it gave me a shock when Jack mentioned the name today.' Alex's tone is suddenly confidential, 'Sash, I ought to let you know what Aled Thomas told me last summer when I was helping unpack some old books he'd bought as a job lot. It's something he found out years ago.'

'Oh! What?'

'He told me how he'd uncovered this old story from the monks of St Dogmaels Abbey; it was something they'd passed down through the centuries. I thought it a lovely tale at the time, nothing more than that you see, now I'm not so sure.'

'Aren't you?'

'I'll tell you what I know, then you'll see what I mean. It seems the monks finally decided to write the tale down. They recorded it in the Aberteifi Chronicle, many years ago. As I said, Aled somehow got hold of a copy.' Alex continues, his voice a mere whisper, 'The story goes that a weird hound was seen in Jerusalem in AD 33. He's there too during the spell of darkness that covers the land from the sixth until the ninth hour, a luminous presence.

Also, the anguished wail of this creature is heard by the Centurion on duty, a key witness of the events. He sees a hound bound past him ... now this is the startling bit, Sash, its fur is gleaming white, so radiant it hurts the Centurion's eyes, and it has crimson ears that glow red like fire coals. Its haunting eyes pierce the heart with their faithfulness.'

'A Hound of Arawn,' Sash murmurs.

'Yeah, it must be. There's more but I can't remember what. I'm sure it's something important. Y'know Gav and me agreed to see Uncle Berwyn in the morning. Of course, I was going to take you with us as well.' He pauses then looking straight into her eyes asks, 'Listen, would you and Nonnie go and see Aled to find out about the Aberteifi Hound as it's called?'

Sash doesn't like the idea of walking past Rough Stone Farm but then thinks, 'I'm not going to let those Vaughan boys frighten me, no way Sasha Littlejohn.' In addition, her inquisitiveness makes her eager to find out everything she can about this

Aberteifi Hound.

'Well?'

'If you weally want me to, yes,' she replies using the little girl voice he finds irresistible.

She can't see his smile but senses it's there as they come together, hugging each other, happy alone, just the two of them under the darkening sky. They stand there embracing, loving each other, while the night grows to a greater depth of blackness broken only by the flickering of far off stars.

CHAPTER 9

Sash isn't sleeping as well as she hoped.

She feels a pulse in her head and knows another nightmare's coming:

… she's five years old in the tiny room of their terrace house. A line of pointed black railings separates her window from the street.

She feels frightened. Mummy isn't there and Daddy's out. She knows she's home alone.

Men arrive, their feet scraping the stone steps. She smells her fear. They might be bad!

The sound of the door knocker rattles through the empty house into her room.

'We're looking for The Searcher, is he at home?' The man's trying to make his voice sound all innocent but he doesn't succeed, underneath she can hear something threatening.

Now, they're at the window, pointing at her to let them in. She can see they're mean but are pretending to be friendly. They try to smile, but as they do so their teeth turn black.

She runs out of her room into the hall.

She can hear the men laughing but not in a nice way. Something is in the letter box. The front door shakes as the letterbox lifts. It looks like their fingernails are growing towards her …

By the time she comes down to breakfast in the morning, the boys have already left for Tirion Mawr and it's not long before she and Nonnie are making their way past Rough Stone Farm to call on Aled Thomas.

The pulse in her head is tenacious.

They enter the village, heading towards the rectory. They catch Jack's rich voice vibrating in song, when they reach Salinas Cottage:

'There is a balm in Gilead
To make the wounded whole
There is a balm in Gilead
To heal the sin-sick soul …'

'A lovely voice and a lovely old man too,' Sash mutters half to herself and half to Nonnie. 'What does balm mean?'

'Balm?'

'Yeah, I heard it in Jack's song.'

'Not sure, but I think it's a kind of healing oil and fragrant too, like perfume; he often sings old slave songs like that, sung by his ancestors.'

'Really sad.'

'Oh!' Nonnie stops in surprise. Parked in front of the rectory there's a red sports car. They peer into the MG Sports impressed by its leather seats, stylish steering wheel and gleaming dashboard. 'Looks like there's a visitor. Shall we knock anyway?'

'Yeah, go on we might as well.'

The square figure of Agnes Thomas answers their knock.

'Oh hello, Agnes,' Nonnie begins brightly, 'is Aled in?'

Sash takes in the brown shoes, black dress, the starched apron with not a speck on it ice-berg white.

'He is Nonnie, but we have an important visitor, just now. Could you call back at eleven o'clock when he should be free? Unless it's very urgent of course, my dear.'

'No, that'll be fine, thanks.'

'And who's your friend now?' Agnes asks, looking at Sasha.

'This is Sash, Alex's friend from London.'

'Pleased to meet you, my dear. Now if you'll excuse me, I must see to our important guest,' she says proudly.

The door closes. The girls trudge back to Gorswen to wait. Luckily for them Enid has an 11.15 appointment in Tal-y-Cafn so can give them a lift.

As the minutes tick by, Sash's headache worsens. Eventually, she says to Nonnie, 'My head's pounding - I really must lie down. Are you okay if I don't come with you after all?'

'No problem, Sash, I'll find out all I can about this Chronicle of Alex's. Now you have a rest, I'll be back in no time.'

Sash hears the door shut and the car driving off. She lies back allowing herself to doze.

Something's wrong!

Sasha doesn't know how long she's slept but there are voices downstairs. Someone in Wellington boots is walking around. The booted intruder runs upstairs. Heavy boots are stomping along the corridor outside her room.

She slips under the eiderdown carefully pulling it tight above her, making it seem like the bed's empty. Her heart is beating so fast she can barely breathe.

Now she can hear a lighter tread on the stair. They're both

upstairs.

Her bedroom door opens. She hears booted feet clump into her room. A drawer scrapes open. Someone is looking through her clothes.

'Found the collar then, have you?'

Her lips clench tight, closed - it's Gareth Vaughan!

'Not yet.'

'You'll not find it among her knickers, will you. Remember what's promised us if we can find the collar too? Get a move on.'

'At least we have the stone. It's well hidden, no-one will ever discover it in all that scree above Tirion Lakes. Even with that dead fir tree marking its place we'd be pushed to get it quickly ourselves.'

'Stop your rabbiting, we're here for the collar, remember. Have you searched next door?'

'No, I've been checking this room first.'

'Come on then. It's not here, is it?'

She can hear them in Alex's room.

Then they pass her door again, tread off downstairs … the house door slams. They've gone, left empty handed.

She lies still, frightened, angry, not daring to move.

Her bedspread is gripped in her hands, it's taut hiding her presence in the room. She knows Gareth Vaughan's looking for a collar, he's working for someone. He stole Jack's stone; it's hidden up in the mountains. She's silent, tense, thinking. 'They slipped up, made a mistake, thought we were all out - but what if they come back to find me here on my own?'

Her window rattles in the wind, she listens, hearing the air swishing through the yard, 'They'll guess I know, if they come back and find me. I must stop them. I can't risk being caught alone. I have to act now, at once.'

It takes her an age to get from her bed to the door. She shudders as it creaks on opening. Out on the landing she can hear the tick of the clock in the room below. Once on the stairs she can see through the small window, out into the yard. She cowers back against the wall, sliding slowly down the stairs, one step at time, hiding from the sight of anyone outside as she descends.

The front door key comes into view, hanging in place beside the picture of Grandfather Lewis, his brown eyes staring out with a surprised, alarmed look. She can hear her blood thudding through her body, she's gripping the wood of the banister alert to the atmosphere in the house. Her fingers feel sticky on the smooth wood as she inches down towards the key.

'If only Nonnie was home, she'd be alright.'

The buzz of the fridge makes her jump. She freezes, her muscles tight ready for flight. 'Come on Sash, you can do this,' she encourages herself.

Trembling, she forces herself down the last of the stairs. She takes the key for the front door from its hook. Pushing it into the lock, she turns it. She feels safer locked in, waiting for the others to come, hoping they will not be long. She sits on the bottom stair, she's left the key in the lock, she waits out of sight ready to let her friends in when they return, willing them to come home soon.

CHAPTER 10

Gavin's leaning against the gate post of Tirion Mawr, panting with Gobaith beside him. 'The Adding-machine's a slow one - needs oiling, does it?'

Alex laughs as he comes up to him and strides past.

Rooks are busy in the grand oaks, 'Aw hawse! Aw hawse!' they seem to cry as they circle and flap.

Berwyn Davies and his dogs greet them on the doorstep. He's a tall man, a little stooped with age but with energy in his bright eyes. 'No Sash today?' he rasps, surprised.

'No, Nonnie and Sash are calling on Aled this morning,' Alex answers.

Berwyn's grey eyebrows rise slightly as if to say, 'Indeed?'

Once in his workshop he says in his gravelly voice, 'We've buried Brutus up by the orchard like I said we would. I'll show you before you leave.'

The boys nod and watch as he fishes a small box from his pocket. It has an acorn carved on its lid. He flicks it open to take a pinch of snuff. He piles this on the side of his fist then draws the dark powder into his nostrils in two sniffs. His eyes water.

Gavin crosses to the window ledge to look closely at the glass paperweight on display, the 'Abergwyngregyn Eye'. It's blue-green, 'gwyrddlas' in Welsh, and filled with bubbles. He knows it's ancient as he looks searchingly into its depths. The word in the family is that those with the old skill can communicate with

…using sight and sound, word and image, but he can see nothing except bubbles and colour and glass. He gazes into its depths with concentration but nothing stirs, there's nothing doing in its silent world that he can see or hear.

Berwyn watches him for a moment. Then he turns to Alex, 'I have to go off tonight and I'm not sure how long I'll be. For obvious reasons I don't want to leave my dogs in the kennels while I'm away.'

Alex nods, sympathetically.

Gavin comes over, looking at Berwyn, wondering what he's going to say.

'Rhian kindly said they can stay with her tonight - but four dogs is rather a lot, do you see?'

'Yes it is,' Gavin agrees.

'Would you boys come over in the morning and take them for a trek on the moor? Once they're well exercised, they'll lie quietly, you see?'

'Of course, that'll be fine, won't it Alex?'

'Absolutely,' Alex agrees, wondering what Sash is going to say.

'Shall we say nine o'clock sharp then?'

They both nod.

'Good, I'll make all the arrangements with Rhian then.'

Alex is ruffling Gob's fur behind his ears in the way he likes.

Berwyn looks on and says, 'Let me take a look at him, will you?' He holds out his hand and Gobaith moves across at the invitation.

None of the other dogs move from their mat but all are watching, while pretending to sleep.

Gob looks into the lively eyes under the greying eyebrows, the encounter brings a leap of recognition and a surge of joy. Then he has to look away. The intensity of the scrutiny is too much for him.

Berwyn is satisfied. He strokes Gobaith's ear saying reassuringly, 'Well old man, well old man - Hen ffrind ffyddlon!'

The look he now gives Alex is calmer, 'He's good and true, I can see that.' Then he mutters something under his breath, which the boys can't hear but Gavin thinks are the words, 'And it's just as well.'

Before they leave, Berwyn takes the boys up to the orchard as promised. Away to the east, the tall tree tops of Bodnant can be seen on the other side of the Conwy. The orchard faces southeast and has a path and wooden fence on its perimeter.

They come to a newly dug mound of earth. At its head, away from the fence, is a wooden stake.

Berwyn says, 'Here lies the noblest Roman of all.'

Alex and Gavin look on sadly.

Gob and the other dogs mingle and sniff around.

'Well, he's got a great resting place,' Alex says, 'with Bodnant and the Conwy to the east and Tirion Lakes and the moor to the west.'

'Yes, indeed he has,' Berwyn agrees while his eyes moisten in the breeze.

CHAPTER 11

'Pity Sasha's feeling unwell, she's great isn't she? I can see you're getting on fine,' Enid adds as she clicks her seat belt together.

'Oh yes,' Nonnie says brightly, 'wrong time of the month for her, that's all Mum.'

'Tell me about it!'

Perched in the front Nonnie glimpses Gareth Vaughan with his brother. They're skulking along the old track to Gorswen that winds along on the other side of the hedge. 'What are they up to?' she thinks to herself irked. Enid's Ford Escort rattles through the farmyard and away.

'Thanks Mum, see you later.'

Enid gives her a swift smile then she's away to Tal-y-Cafn for her appointment with old Mrs Griffiths, the Post.

Nonnie turns towards the rectory, quickly noting the red MG has gone. She trots lightly up the steps and knocks.

Agnes Thomas opens the door. 'Nice and prompt, my dear, come along, will you? Would you like a cup of tea?'

Nonnie follows her into the kitchen saying, 'That'd be nice.'

'I'll put the kettle on, my dear.'

'I see your visitor has gone,' Nonnie comments by way of polite conversation.

'Yes he has. A very good young man, Michael George from

Aberystwyth, and he's offering to pay for new carpet in our little church here.'

'Wow, that's generous,' Nonnie says in surprise, 'but he's not a local, is he?'

'No, my dear, he's from Aberystwyth.'

There's a pause while Agnes pours the tea. She's in a good mood after the visit of Mr George and disposed to talk.

Nonnie's curious. 'How does he know about our church?'

Agnes smiles complacently, 'Oh it's because of Aled. You know how clever he is?'

'Yeah, he knows loads.'

'He helped this Mr George, you see, with some old manuscript no-one could decipher. Aled just happened to be in Aberystwyth seeing one of his old friends from years back. Well, they got talking, the manuscript was mentioned. Could Aled make anything of it? Of course, he could and did. So this young man asked if there was anything he could do for Aled. He was so insistent, Aled eventually remembered the church carpet! I've been telling him for years that it's tatty and needs to be replaced.'

'It's not that bad. I wouldn't call it tatty,' Nonnie says thinking of the plush, crimson carpet in their church,

'Well, my dear, you can take it from me, it's passed its best so needs replacing, of course. Anyway, Mr George came over this spring, that's when Aled introduced me to him, such a polite young man!' She pauses, enjoying her recollection of this smart, young gentleman.

Nonnie sips her tea waiting for Agnes to finish.

'Well, Aled let me take him to the church on my own to show him the carpet. Mr George agreed with me and offered to pay for the whole thing himself!' Agnes took a long breath, drawing her shoulders back to look at Nonnie in triumph.

'Very generous, I must say.' From nowhere she suddenly feels uncomfortable. Perhaps she shouldn't have left Sash alone in the house? She senses something isn't right, it makes her uneasy.

'Well, my dear, I see you've finished your tea. Nice to have a chat but I've work to do you know. Cleaning and dusting today, it is.'

'Yes, sorry to take up so much of your time. Is …?'

'Oh, I forgot to tell you, Aled's been called away. Before he left, he gave me this note, sorry my dear.' She stands up, taking a folded piece of paper down from the shelf behind her and handing it to Nonnie.

Taking the folded paper Nonnie reads:

Dear young Ladies,

I am sorry to give you a wasted journey this morning, but I have an unexpected appointment and will be away for the day.

Please call again at 10 am tomorrow when I shall be free to see you, I promise.

Sincerely as ever,

Aled T

'He says to call again tomorrow at ten and he'll see us then,' she says feeling strangely relieved, yet miffed at the wasted time, returning home having found out nothing at all, feeling it's been a disappointing morning.

'Yes, I know, my dear.'

'Okay, see you then, thanks for the tea.'

'You're welcome, my dear.'

The words are hardly out of Agnes's mouth before Nonnie's

gone, hurrying home, buzzing along the road.

CHAPTER 12

The phone rings. It's Nonnie who takes the call.

Sash is sitting on the high-backed settle beside the fire, her head resting on Alex's shoulder. She's allowed Gob up beside her, he's lying contentedly, his head on her lap.

Gavin looks up as Nonnie returns, 'Well?'

'Oh, that was Mum. Mrs Griffith the Post has got very high blood pressure so Mum's going to stay with her tonight - she was just phoning to make sure we're okay so I said no probs.'

'That rather decides things for us doesn't it?' Alex exclaims. 'Thanks to Sash we know they're after this collar whatever it is. Also, we've a good idea where Jack's stone is hidden. That's really something - imagine Jack's face if we can get it back for him!'

'The Vaughan boys are to blame,' Gavin butts in.

'Yeah, we know about them for sure,' Alex agrees. 'What do we do now?'

The others all look at him, waiting to hear what he'll say.

'I think our best plan is for Gav and me to go off to Rhian's tomorrow as arranged. Then we can search for the stone while we're on the moor with Berwyn's dogs.' He puts a hand on Sasha's shoulder, 'Sash, I know you're short of energy, you've probably still got a bit of a headache as well, but do you think you could go with Nonnie to meet with Aled?'

'If I sleep all right, I should be okay. Can you let Gobaith sleep in mine tonight? He's like a warm, cuddly teddy, aren't you Gob?' she replies, stroking his neck.

'Course you can have him,' Alex smiles, catching her eye as he speaks, 'I'm thinking you should tell Aled what we know about the theft. You'd better mention this collar the Vaughan brothers are after as well. He'll know what's best to do.'

'But won't that mean they've got to go past Rough Stone Farm on their own?' Gavin objects.

'Yeah, you're right. That's not so good, is it?'

'We aren't scared of the Vaughans. They were looking for this collar thing. They won't dare hurt us! Nonnie exclaims.

'Tell you what - why don't you take Gobaith with you?'

'I'd like that,' Sash says. 'He'll be our minder,' she laughs.

Soon Gavin and the girls are preparing for bed. Alex can hear them walking about upstairs, calling Gob from room to room. When the patter of feet settles, he sits by the fire. There's a low hiss from the burning wood, beyond a night time hush descends, silence shrouds the building.

He looks deep into the devouring flames. His thoughts are on the stone face: so suddenly discovered after being hidden for ages - now taken, stolen, thieved by neighbours! The idea of the robbery marks his thoughts, dirty, not right. He feels the challenge, an unknown conflict, a testing time coming, approaching. He's alone, on the alert, ready for an ambush or worse.

His senses are alive, tasting the air, aware of the sinister being that's come. He's wary, feeling its dark presence. It is near, waiting for its chance, intending harm, plotting destruction.

Lurking just out of sight, but close, is something malevolent. Cold fingers reach for his heart. Fierce, cruel, it's trying to enter, force its way in - he must not let it into his mind. He knows it is desperate for the key, for a way in ... also ... Can it feed off his fear? Hell - it's feeding off his terror!

'Think of something else, man,' it's Jack's voice in his head.

Alex can almost see his American friend, Jack Achebe, he pictures the old man's face, crinkled in laughter. He thinks of the river, the maiden singing ... the bubbles in the water. He recalls sunny days, sitting with Sash above the Tirion lakes ... the ravens in flight. He thinks of Gobaith jumping ... of dust moving in a shaft of sunlight.

The threat withdraws, the ice around his heart thaws. Alex senses it is still out there, it's nearby in the darkness waiting, waiting for him to drop his guard.

There is a brackish smell in the room, so he gives the fire a poke, allowing it to breathe, a flurry of sparks, followed by a flickering flame which licks the logs once more.

Once in bed, fearing another attack he keeps a protective wall around him, a bright ring to keep him safe: honey, flowers in the hay meadow, swallows in flight ...he fences himself in with warm thoughts waiting for sleep to come but every time he puts up a thought, darkness obliterates another part of the circle.

He's too tired.

The cold mass is back, seeping through the cracks in his fence. He's exhausted, his mind is becoming slow, almost stubborn. The room feels strangely empty without the weight of Gobaith on his feet. He feels hopeless, lost, unable to fight it any longer ... just in time he escapes into the dark forest of slumber:

As he walks, voices call and whine, *The Stone! The Collar! The Whistle!* He notices how Gobaith is beside him, paying no attention to these cries but padding steadfastly forward, onwards, further into the pool of black.

He realises with surprise it's Gob leading him.

Out of the darkness he hears a voice lisp, *Give me the stone, boy.*

Gobaith doesn't hesitate; on he pads parting the darkness as he goes.

Alex hurries after him, his legs aren't working properly, he's struggling to keep up.

A high-pitched shriek vibrates in his right ear, *Boy, give me the coll-ar!*

He notices Gobaith!
Coat gleaming…

Dazzling white in the dark…

Ears glowing… on fire!

Whistles are blowing. Leaves, twigs are flurrying around, a voice, a thunderclap booms, *Boy, hand me that whistle!*

He looks up as a blinding flash sears his eyes, he's falling, blacking out, whirling down, round, falling down …

Alex sits up, his heart thumping inside his ribcage. The room is dark, black, heavy on his shoulders. He doesn't know how long he's slept; he can hear the wind in the oaks above his window. Again, he feels this menace, lurking, close. He understands! He has to move now, take action, prevent it from taking hold.

He struggles up. He wants to look into the night sky, so flings back the curtains. There! On the window ledge, just outside, sits a massive bird.

Its baleful, unblinking eye fixes on him. It clicks its hooked beak once before swooping off into the dark.

'Only a buzzard driven here to shelter from the storm, poor thing,' he thinks, putting aside its cruel beak, the cold look in its eye.

The wind shrieks an octave higher while below comes a rumbling grumble of thunder - storm clouds are crashing high above the house.

Flash!

'One, two, three, four, five -'

'The storm's five miles away,' he thinks, 'it's probably what woke me.'

He snuggles back into bed, pulling the blankets tightly round.

In a moment of inspiration, he thinks of Little Sal. Here she comes. She's moving along the school corridor on her crutch. He's back at the beginning of the January term, the cancer that began in her leg is spreading but she's fearless. As they pass, she flashes him a brilliant smile - he's not alone - it's uplifting, comforting, allowing him to fall asleep safe in the company of his courageous friend.

CHAPTER 13

'The Adding-machine's a slow one!

The Adding-machine lost its fuse!

In any race it's sure to lose!'

Gavin chants in victory as he waits for Alex.

There's a slight scuffle. Gavin finds himself bent double. He feels Alex's arm tighten around his neck; for all his effort he's powerless under the controlled pressure.

Alex looks down on the mop of fair hair in his arm. He searches for Gavin's mouth, smothering it with his free hand. 'What's happened to your voice, Gav? I like a song - sing me another one if you can!' Laughing loudly, he releases his hold to rush ahead, arriving first at Rhian's front door.

'Come on in, boys! There's a piece of chocolate cake before you start,' Rhian says, throwing the door wide.

As they finish the last crumbs of her homemade cake she says, 'And Alex, before you go, your Uncle Berwyn has told me to give you this whistle.'

Alex feels a tingle of excitement race through him. In his head he recalls the echo of the voices from his nightmare, *Give me the whistle, boy!*

In her hand is a whistle fashioned out of animal horn. A thin, leather thong passes through the carved eye at the whistle's head. Alex has often seen this whistle hanging from his uncle's neck.

'Mind that you take good care of it,' she warns. 'It's old and very valuable I dare say. You couldn't make something like it today. We don't have the craftsmen anymore, see.'

She holds it for a moment more, 'All his dogs know its note and will hear it from miles away. He's trained them to it and they're sure to come to you if you blow it, see?'

Alex feels the smooth surface of the horn as he takes it. It's cool. He caresses it in his palm, feeling his way along the lined grooves and ridges, before slipping the thong over his head.

'Take care today boys, the Postman's Path will be slippery after all that rain in the night. Did you hear the storm at Gorswen?'

'What storm? I must've slept right through it', Gavin answers.

'Well take care, it's still rumbling around I dare say. Come with me, I'll let the dogs out,' and she leads them to the lean-to at the back of the cottage, smiling as she opens the door to the dogs.

Out they bound, giving the boys a joyous welcome. Punch rushes up and down with his brown tail pumping, while Chisel, the other spaniel, keeps close to the boys. The two labs, Piper and Spray trot about wagging their tails powerfully.

The liveliness of the dogs contrasts with the brooding atmosphere.

Grey mist hangs over the mountain tops. The stream below Rhian's cottage has become a sinuous creature, thrashing its brown body down the hill to its hissing big brother in the valley below.

Dampness hangs over Tirion Mawr and the oaks at the back door stand silent, except for the drip, drip, drip falling on the ground.

Alex feels the dampness reaching inside him like a clammy

hand.

He's grateful for the cheerful company of Gav who is jogging around, chivvying the dogs as he goes.

Alex scans the larch trees growing on the lower hillside. He senses something - there is something hateful tracking them - he can feel its brooding presence.

They disturb the rooks, who rise from their treetop towers crying, 'Haw!, Haw!, Haw!' as they circle and flap.

Gavin looks up at them, his hand over his eyes for a clearer view. Alex strides forward, keeping his eyes down, away from the birds. He's clasping the whistle, making sure it cannot be seen.

The boys are soon on the ancient cart track skirting the side of the hill. It's sheltered by hawthorn growing along each side like twin sisters, pointing their spiky fingers accusingly at the mist-covered hills.

Soon they reach higher ground where the path narrows. They plan to walk this Postman's Path, expecting to arrive at the dead fir tree by noon.

The path is steep and slippery.

It climbs round the hill like a creeper but, in places, there's a long, dangerous stretch between footholds. They tread carefully as it is sheer, so steep in fact that a fall would be fatal.

Below them sit tidy little farmhouses.

First, they look down on Brynonn. The red Massey-Fergusson in the yard looks like a child's toy. The whitewashed house and neat green fields give a sense of order under the dark sky.

Alex stops for a moment to absorb the view.

His eye swings down the valley, taking in the river, the woods and the tarmac road with a dotted white line down its centre -

all seems calm but he feels the threat is close, senses he's being watched.

He looks down at Spray, noting her raised hackles.

Then he's off after Gav up the slippery path, treading warily on the wet slate and loose shale. Piper and the two spaniels are in front, but Gavin is on their heels, setting Alex a lively pace as always.

There's a long way to go. They have to climb round the hill and then drop down to Tirion Lakes, before beginning the final ascent straight up the mountainside to the edge of the moor.

From across the valley comes a troubled rumbling, a warning of bad weather circling.

CHAPTER 14

The cagoule-clad figures of Nonnie and Sash lope along the road to Rough Stone Farm. Their heads are close together so they can chat quietly as they go.

It's a dismal morning. A rusty tractor sits abandoned in the yard, beside it is a coil of discarded barbed-wire. The corrugated-iron barn contains bales of straw, some appearing mouldy. Water is sliding, spilling down where the gutter has broken. A pitchfork lies on the ground, its worm-eaten handle covered in red sheep-dye, nearby is an enamel bowl, its wet base covered in weed.

'I pity the animals on this farm, just look at the mess!' Sash says crossly. She casts a furtive glance at the curl of smoke leaking from the single chimney.

Someone is in.

A washing line droops in the damp. A pair of black overalls hanging there seem to her like the grim figure of a corpse. She shudders as she thinks of the intruders of the previous day. 'I don't like this place,' she whispers to Nonnie and holds Gobaith's lead tightly.

'They're not entirely bad, you know, Mum visits often because of Idris. He's their crippled father, those boys tend him. You know they watch over him with fierce pride,' Nonnie explains, allowing Sash an insight into how Enid is such a vital person to the locals.

As they cross the bridge to pass Riverside Cottage, their spirits lift. They climb up through the village and arrive at the rectory, Persondy, in good time. The house has a high hedge in front. In its centre is a gateway arch over which wild dog-roses grow.

The door opens to Nonnie's knock. Agnes greets them, 'On time that's good, come along with you, he's a busy man so we mustn't keep him waiting, come along now.'

Once inside she turns to the girls saying, 'Give me those wet things, I'll hang them here for you in the dry and you can leave your dog, Gobaith is it?'

Sash nods giving her the lead,

'He can stay out in the back with me.' She hangs up their coats, then wipes her feet pointedly on the mat muttering, 'Clean and tidy is best; dust settles on the idle.'

Nonnie glances at Sash to share a smirk.

Agnes notices their smiles and says sharply, 'Right then, don't be bringing any mess in with you. There's good girls.'

They file through the spotless kitchen. A rush mat is placed before the range for Gobaith, who settles himself quickly, before Agnes leads the girls along the polished tiles to Aled's study.

Aled's bending over a large book. He has a magnifying glass in his hand and is peering through it in concentrated intensity.

As they enter he looks up and beams at the girls, 'Good morning, ladies. Come on in and take a seat, will you? Not for keeps,' he laughs, 'just for sitting.'

They settle into the chairs beside him while Agnes withdraws, closing the door behind her.

'Has anyone ever told you the story of the absent minded vicar?'

'No, we've never heard it,' Nonnie answers sweetly.

'Indeed,' the Rev says looking pleased, 'well let me tell you it.'

"The absent-minded vicar paused for a moment to have a chat with his parishioner, see? And he asked her, 'By the way, when did you last see me?'

'Last Sunday,' the parishioner answers.

And he says, 'Oh good, so I went to church then!'"

On the other side of the door Agnes can hear laughter and her husband booming away as he entertains his guests. Then she slips away back to her own tasks.

The girls are laughing happily. There's a warmth about Aled that's put them at their ease.

He raises his massive hands and smooths his dark hair, which like his eyebrows, is flecked with grey. 'Now then, ladies, tell me what I can do for you?' he says invitingly.

'I'd like to tell you what happened yesterday, when I came here and Sash stayed at home because she'd a bad headache.' Nonnie looks from Sash to Aled for a moment, 'You see Mum was out on a call to Mrs. Griffith the Post and because she had high blood pressure Mum stayed over to keep an eye on her.'

'That was good of her, we're lucky with our district nurse here, I dare say,' Aled responds.

Nonnie smiles her agreement quickly, 'Anyway Sash was up in the bedroom having a nap when she was disturbed by intruders. One of them was wearing boots and she heard him clumping upstairs and Sash managed to hide herself under her bedspread.'

Aled Thomas knits his brows.

'They were obviously looking for something and searching all the rooms. Also, Sash overheard them talking about the stone they'd stolen and hidden, above Tirion Lakes.'

'What were they looking for?'

'A collar and I recognised one of them from his voice,' Sash answers.

'Who was it?'

'Gareth Vaughan,' Sash and Nonnie speak together.

Nonnie's face is flushed. She can see Aled's looking troubled.

'So Gareth's taken Jack's stone, he's hidden it? Above Tirion Lakes, you say?'

'Yes.'

'Well that's very useful information - so we've a chance of getting Jack's stone back - they were looking for a collar you say?'

'Yes, searching everywhere for it.'

'Do you know what it is or where it is?'

'No, we haven't a clue,' Nonnie says, looking at Sash and shrugging.

'Yeah, I've no idea what it can be,' Sash agrees, 'but do you know something? I've found myself searching for it too, I've always been curious that way. I like finding old things; I've always been like that.'

'Indeed, have you Sasha?' Aled asks with a smile.

'Yes, I get it from my dad, I think. Before he died, we liked going to Charmouth in Dorset by the sea. We spent time there fossil hunting, while mum sunbathed and Little Sal played in the pools.'

'Indeed. When does Enid get home now?' Aled asks, turning from Sasha to Nonnie.

'She should be back this afternoon at the latest.'

Aled looks at Sasha and then back at Nonnie. He says decisively, 'I think it's best that we wait to speak with her before we act on this one. You're absolutely right to tell me now since your mother's away but let's wait and see what she says - the Vaughans are your neighbours - it's best to be careful, see?'

Sash glances at Nonnie.

He reads her look and asks, 'Is there something more?'

'Oh, yes actually,' Sash says, 'Alex was telling me the other day how he was helping you last summer when you told him about the Abertivvy Chronicle and the …'

'I think Sash means the Aberteifi Chronicle,' Nonnie clarifies.

Aled nods, his dark eyes are fixed on the girls because he is listening, listening to their every word.

'Sorry,' Sash says before continuing, 'anyway Alex told me about this strange hound seen in AD 33, in Jerusalem, when darkness covered the land, seen by the Centurion who described its fur as gleaming white but that it had red, glowing ears.'

'A hound of Arawn.' Nonnie adds wistfully.

'But Alex can't remember the rest of the story. He's asked me to find it out if I can,' Sash stops, looking up at Aled for an answer.

'It's an old place, sacked by the Vikings in 988, let me see,' and he reaches down to the bottom drawer of his desk taking a box-file out and flicking the lid open

The girls lean forward to see the sheaf of papers he is picking up. They can read the words *'St Dogmaels Abbey'* on the front cover.

Aled turns the pages carefully, then stops to read for a moment. 'Indeed the Centurion speaks of the hound's haunting, brown eyes that pierce the heart,' he says without looking up.

'Oh yes, Alex told me that bit too.'

'He has a good memory, that boy, now let me see,' and he reads some more in silence. Then he looks up at Sash and then at Nonnie too. 'There is something more but perhaps I should read you the passage in the chronicler's own words?'

The girls agree.

Aled begins reading in a slightly awed tone:

'I, the Centurion on duty, saw all this. The innocent one cried out, then his head dropped forward in death. The wind whistled, the earth shook on its foundations. The night shrieked. I heard the long wail of a hound, haunting, strange. The night was split by a fork of light; immediately the crashing boom of war could be heard in the air above.

Rushing, panting, sobbing - the bounding creature loomed out of the dark. Its fur was a gleaming white; its crimson ears glowed. Its eyes were seared with pain, around its neck burnt a collar of love. My eyes stung, I had to look away.'

Aled puts the papers back, 'And that is all there is.'

'What do you think the collar of love is?' Sash asks, 'I think that's the bit Alex forgot.'

'Indeed, I've thought about it a lot, you see? The clergy often wear a white dog-collar around the neck,' he says, touching his collar with his hands. ' It's a sign of our devotion to the Lord, you see?'

'I get that,' Sash says.

'I suppose the chronicler intended it as a sign of the hound's pure devotion. Mind you, there's nothing about this hound anywhere Matthew, Mark and Luke all mention the Centurion on duty and John mentions the soldiers who were present.'

He shrugs his shoulders as he adds,' A lot was destroyed by the Vikings so you never know but I expect the monks of the abbey embroidered things a little, don't you?'

Abruptly the door swings open as a flustered Agnes Thomas hurries in exclaiming, 'Dear! Dear! Dear!'

'What's the matter, Agnes?' he asks kindly.

'I cannot say how it happened but the dog has gone!' she exclaims.

'What?' Sash asks in alarm.

'I left him in front of the range to go upstairs to do some ironing but when I came down, just a moment ago, the kitchen door was open and the dog was gone.'

Sash is feeling alarmed. She senses something is not right but Nonnie beside her is looking okay.

'I expect the wind blew the door open and Gobaith went back to Gorswen looking for Alex,' Nonnie says.

'Do you?' Sash asks, thinking that perhaps her imagination has made her fear the worst when it is really nothing more than Nonnie says.

'Seems the most likely explanation, Sash, doesn't it?' Nonnie reassures her. ' I think we'd better hurry home and find him though.'

'Indeed, so you should,' Aled agrees.

The girls pick up their coats and begin to leave.

Aled calls after them, 'Be sure to phone me when you reach Gorswen if Gobaith isn't there!'

'Thanks we will!' Nonnie shouts as they hurry off into the storm.

CHAPTER 15

The race is on to the lifeless fir tree.

The early morning mist has lifted. Even at this height, there is little breeze and thick clouds shroud the mountain-tops. Gav is comfortably ahead of his dark haired cousin. He holds his anorak in the crook of his arm, his fair hair damp with perspiration.

Gav begins to wind his way up the stone strewn slope. He keeps his eyes fixed on the ground in the hope of spotting the stone. He knows it's here somewhere, but has little hope - there are hundreds of stones scattered around! He stops a moment and gives Alex a cheeky wave. Except for Spray, the dogs are above him, from time to time their pattering feet dislodge a flurry of shale that comes flying down past his boots. The spaniels are hunting constantly but every so often Piper comes back to check on his progress.

Alex stops for a breather and looks up. He can see that Gav is beginning the steeper part of the climb, 'Nimble as a young goat, I'll never catch him now,' he thinks to himself.

Gav is taking extra care. The path is slippery and he knows his cousin is below him. He has to reach for footholds and handholds and has to be careful not to dislodge any rocks that might fall. He takes deep, controlled breaths between movements now he's on sheer rock. He finds his anorak an encumbrance, so stops and puts it back on despite the sweat streaming from the pores of his head.

The dogs know their way up the mountain. Piper is sitting on a flat surface, shielded from view by rushes, some ten yards above the climbing Gavin. The spaniels are bounding through the heather beyond the rushes, enjoying the freedom of the moor.

Gav pulls himself up over the last sheet of slate and flings himself down next to Piper, victorious.

The dead fir tree is some twenty or so yards above him up the scree from here but he has reached the top of the Postman's Path and won. He and Piper wait for Alex and Spray. He can just see Alex's dark hair bobbing into view as he climbs - now you see it now you don't.

Gav allows his eyes to roam. Below him the pine forest is a spikey green sea. High in the sky and difficult to see under the blackening clouds, a solitary buzzard circles round scanning the ground. Beneath it the little country road, black and neat, twists its way down the valley.

Then, Alex is beside him, breathing heavily.

Gav gives him a toothy grin, putting his arm around Spray in greeting.

Looking down together on the climb they just conquered, they pause feeling triumphant, before making the last few yards to the dead tree. The fir stands tall and grey. Its two main branches are like arms reaching out to embrace all comers. To its right and left are charred stumps. They are all that remain after lightning struck the three pines, many years ago.

A violent storm seems about to erupt. Gav looks uneasily at the threatening sky.

Alex is searching methodically. He's walking around the old tree stumps in a widening arc and turning over bigger stones as he comes across them, hoping to find Jack's ancient stone with its carving of Aenlic Angharad.

A large white boulder catches his eye. It's flecked with black and reminds him of ones he has seen in a rockery. He glances up at the angry sky and as he does so, a solitary buzzard circles into his vision. It has climbed with them and he watches it, idly.

The buzzard begins to gyrate. It speeds round, ever faster, like water emptying out of a bath. Now it is like a great whirlpool in the sky, it's hurtling round, faster, faster, faster.

Alex feels dizzy. His head spins, 'What's happening to me?' his question comes too late, he's twisted out of the light into a place of shadows.

All is dark. He is in a new dimension where the silence is absolute. Gavin and the dogs are gone, obliterated by the dark. He is on his own.

Slowly, his senses grow accustomed to his new world and he begins to make out shapes. He can just see the dead fir tree, which is glowing faintly. He is conscious of the whistle still hanging round his neck, and clasps it in his left hand for reassurance.

Below and beyond the fir to the east, in the distance, he can see a faint light. 'What can it be?' he wonders.

A cry of pain shivers on the air from the valley in the east, the sound has arrived after the light and he realises both emanate from the same source. The cry cuts into him and he reaches for understanding as he trembles, 'Sash?'

Moments later a screaming jet of hate hits him. The putrid smell of carrion flings him to his knees. Something huge, something seeking him, knows where he is.

Back it comes, stealthily this time.

His mind fills with lethargy. Despair seeks to place its slimy hand over his mouth. Hopelessness fills his nostrils. He finds the stench unbearable, shakes his head to twist himself free.

I only want the whistle, comes the shrill whine in his ear. *Throw it to me; it's easy; let me have it; leave the whistle with me.*

He's tempted to cooperate, anything to be free of the hideous presence beside him, but the words have a false note so he snaps his mind away, shaking his head.

Give it to me, Alex.

The tone is smoother, more persuasive, *Give it to me, Alex, you do not need it anymore.*

His left hand begins to move from the whistle towards the thong, from the hard horn to the soft leather.

The words have a hypnotic quality as they repeat, *Give it to me, Alex, you do not need it anymore. Give it to me, Alex, you do not need it anymore. Give ....*

He begins to lift the thong carefully over his head.

A tone of oozing pleasure creeps into the words, *... you do not need it anymore. Give it to me, Alex ...*

He pauses. In a recess in his mind he hears the echo of Rhian saying something ... he's catching it ... she's saying ... 'Mind you take care of it.'

The persuasive voice continues, *Give it to me, Alex, you do not need it anymore.*

How easy and pleasant, it seems to Alex to do what the voice urges him.

'It's old and very valuable I dare say,' Rhian's words continue. 'We don't have the craftsmen any more, see?'

Alex is puzzled. The conflicting words confuse him.

'All his dogs know its note and will hear it from miles away.'

Give it to me, Alex ... but a note of impatience has crept in.

Alex hesitates. He's unsure so begins putting the thong back over his head to think but it's heavy now, a real weight to lift. He has to use both hands to push it up and over. It's hard like a chain on the back of his neck.

CHAPTER 16

Nonnie and Sash hurry out through the gateway of Persondy. They pause momentarily at Salinas Cottage but there's no sign of Gob so they carry on, hurrying urgently down through the village until they reach Riverside Cottage.

'I bet he's gone home,' Nonnie says hopefully.

'Yeah,' Sash answers, gripping the empty lead in her pocket.

The sky's darkening by the second; their spirits, already low, sink as they approach Rough Stone Farm.

As they come within sight of the farm buildings, Nonnie grabs Sasha's arm, 'Look at that!'

The girls stare in astonishment at the red MG Sports - the car they saw so recently at the rectory. It looks out of place somehow.

The dominating figure of Gareth Vaughan looms over the car. He's in a furious conversation with the driver.

The girls come nearer drawing his attention; he looks up in triumph. 'If it isn't Miss Hoity-toity then. You need to take better care of your doggie. He's been a naughty boy he has,' he sneers pointing along the fence.

They look in horror at a rusty bar sunk into the ground. They gasp. Gobaith is tied to it by a coil of barbed wire cruelly twisted round his neck. His white fur is bloodstained; his head is forced low.

Gareth leans back against the gatepost, smirking. His chipped tooth, sharp, jagged, gives him a menacing savagery - he'll smash them to pulp if challenged.

The girls surge past the car rushing right up to him. Nonnie is shouting, 'You bully! You're nothing but a cowardly bully, Gareth Vaughan!'

Sash is overwhelmed by fury. Her arms hail down on him as she tries to beat him with her clenched fists.

He wards her blows away easily. Then his attitude hardens, a cruel scowl disfigures his face. Malice flickers from his eyes. He catches Sasha's left wrist high in the air. He holds it firmly for a moment, triumphant. He'll teach her. Then he brings it crashing down onto the top bar of the gate.

The metal clangs loudly before Sasha's high-pitched scream rends the air. He throws her roughly to the floor, at his feet.

'You can keep your dirty, little fists to yourself,' Gareth spits at her.

Nonnie squats down beside her friend. She takes the injured hand in hers and asks, 'Can you move your fingers?' She can see that several layers of skin are torn off where blood's running down the wrist.

Sash begins to move her fingers, 'I'm okay, thanks,' she answers tearfully.

Michael George has been looking urgently under his car seat. He eases himself out of the car, hurrying over to them, 'I think this'll help,' he says soothingly, and flips open the plastic catches of a 'First Aid Box.'

His cool hand takes Sasha's wrist and she catches a whiff of aftershave. She glances through her tears at him, giving a watery smile.

Sasha sits passively, while he applies the antiseptic cream lightly to her cuts.

The cream acts fast, taking some of the heat out of the pain throbbing in her knuckles.

He unwinds some lint bandage and cuts it neatly. Then he bandages her hand firmly.

His hands are clean and strong. Sash notices a ruby glinting in the middle of a signet ring sitting snugly on the little finger of his hand. She notes how rounded his finger nails are and how the backs of his hands are tanned.

He swings her up to her feet, 'There we are,' he says gently.

'Th - anks,' she sobs.

In the next instant he turns on Gareth, speaking with quiet authority, 'Look here, Gareth Vaughan, you cannot behave like that you know?'

Gareth stands his ground, scowling.

'You assaulted this girl so I'll have to inform the police, do you understand?'

Gareth shakes his head, 'It was self-defence she was attacking me!' he says fiercely.

'Well you can explain that to the police, can't you?' Sasha's fair-haired champion says smoothly.

'Glyn the Police will see things differently, see?' Gareth says defiantly.

'You'll be prosecuted too, for what you've done to that poor dog. It's against the law to treat animals with savage cruelty like that!' Michael George says emphatically. 'You're for it, you know that don't you?' His final question is chucked contemptuously at Gareth.

Gareth is staring at the ground but he looks up at this with wild eyes. He is looking for something to strike as his temper rises again.

Michael George stands waiting.

Gareth looks at him, weighing the situation, wary now, "I've got my rights, see? I have to protect my livestock don't I?' Now he is defiant again as he blurts out, 'I could 've shot it for chasing our sheep, that's lenient, that is,' jerking his head towards the snared Gobaith.

'He'd never chase sheep!' Nonnie shouts, 'You're a dirty liar! Just you wait, I'm reporting you to the RSPCA.'

'You'd better free the dog at once,' Michael George cuts in crisply.

'I wanted to teach 'em a lesson, see?' Gareth sneers. 'Hoity-toity there's got to learn hasn't she? Coming here with her nose in the air, telling us how to look after our Meg when she can't even control her own dog.'

'Go on, free it now,' Michael George tells him.

Gobaith gives a low growl as Gareth steps over to him.

The dog cannot move but continues to growl as Gareth takes a pair of worn wire-cutters from his coat. He stoops down to the wire, a vein swells in his forehead, a snip is heard as the cutters bite, freeing the wire from the rusty bar holding it.

Gob doesn't move. A circlet of barbed wire is still twisted around his neck. He has learnt even the slightest movement causes the barbs to dig painfully into his flesh. He lies still but his low growling continues like distant, reverberating thunder.

Storm clouds are gathering and Sasha feels giddy, 'Probably delayed shock,' she says to herself.

Her perspective changes, she's dizzy in the darkening

atmosphere, it's as if she's looking through an eerie, liquid sky. She feels like she is peering down a microscope into water.

The two men before her appear like elongated tadpoles, black, slimy.

Gobaith is glistening. Alert - he sits upright with his ears pricked. His senses are straining in the direction of the high ground, he's looking towards the moor, away in the west.

The wire coiled about his neck is shining with blinding intensity. His white fur gleams and his brown patches glow a wonderful crimson. Before her eyes he grows to a grand height, towering over the tadpole-like men. The collar around his neck is as bright as the flash from a welder's rod, a blinding white light.

As if from another dimension, she hears the faintest, most exquisite music. It's like the tinkle of a bell, softly ringing, then it sounds like a mountain stream, running pure and clear, and then it is sheer joy like the laugh of a tiny child.

Gobaith hears it. His ear prick, his head turns towards the sound. The next instant, he springs forward, a massive springer spaniel: high, graceful, so majestic. Away he bounds in huge leaps; away to the west he runs.

Sasha watches him as if she's seeing a slow motion action replay but, as she does so, she begins to fall. She's cushioned by smooth, soapy bubbles. She's touching rose-scented tresses, the sweetest song fills her ears.

Collapsing, unconscious, Sash lies in the mud beside the fence.

CHAPTER 17

As soon as the girls leave, Aled Thomas hurries to the phone. He dials quickly; it's a number he knows well. Then he's listening, hearing it connect with Tirion Mawr.

The rasping voice of Berwyn answers.

'The Reader is calling, the Reader is calling,' Aled repeats urgently.

'The Keeper is answering, the Keeper is answering,' comes the rasping reply.

'Glad you're home my friend, I'm calling a meeting of the Trifolium. The long expected time is upon us, fast upon us, I should say.'

'I'm back early since there was a problem with the slate. I was annoyed at the time but now I see it was fortune - something greater than us at work perhaps,' the Keeper rasps. 'Come to Tirion as soon as you can. The Eye will be ready'

The Reader replaces the receiver and calls to Agnes as he takes his coat, 'I'm off to Tirion Mawr, if Nonnie Lewis phones tell her to call me there, will you?' Aled hurries out, quickly pulling his coat on, as he leaves. Then he heads straight to Salinas Cottage to meet up with Jack and take him to the urgent meeting.

The Keeper wastes no time. He places a gate-leg table in the centre of the room. From the bottom drawer of his work desk, he takes a green cloth and spreads it on the table. At its centre is a yellow circle, like a sun. Next he carries the Abergwyngregyn

Eye over from the windowsill, positions it carefully on the yellow circle and fits it exactly on top of the yellow sun.

Above the eye, depicted on the cloth is a white dove, written above it in red embroidery are the words: 'Love, Joy, Peace.' Just below the dove are three more words, stitched in red: 'Patience, Faith, Courage.'

Below the eye, stitched in black thread is written, clear to see: 'Deep within them I will plant my law, writing it on their hearts.'

Along the bottom of the cloth is a line of finely embroidered red flowers with fluffy, spear-shaped heads, buzzing just above them are a few bees. Hidden in the flowers is what seems to be a green-eyed raven.

The Keeper checks the table, examines the cloth and stares into the depth of the glass. Then he looks up satisfied, he's ready. He hears the approach of a car and knows the others have come.

'Gee bud, were we lucky man your slate delivery was cancelled,' the Finder says by way of greeting as he enters the house.

'A lucky chance, possibly,' the Keeper rasps. 'It's all prepared, we'd better get started right away, there's not a moment to lose.'

Once around the table they link hands to form a ring. Before they start the Reader says, 'We believe the Searcher has come among us, the Finder was the first to sense it and my reading of the signs confirms it now.'

'If so, this may be a time of trial, a time of greatest hazard,' the Keeper rasps.

They begin to move slowly around the table in a clockwise direction, as they circle the Finder's strong singing reverberates in the room:

'There is a balm in Gilead
To make the wounded whole

There is a balm in Gilead
To heal the sin-sick soul ...'

Round and round the table they go, their eyes fixed on the glass at its centre, Gradually the bubbles clear. Then in the blue-green of the eye they see the moor, the dead fir tree with, just beside it, the figure of Alex.

There is something else there as they look: a figure lurks very near to the boy.

For a moment the Finder's voice falters, a collective gasp is heard as their hands tighten. The Reader groans - 'The Sleeker!'

The enemy hasn't noticed them because it's so fixated on Alex, on the whistle hanging around his neck, but they know it to be the sightless Sleeker, a huge adversary, one they could never hope to challenge, a demon from the depths of Hell... an enslaver.

As they circle round, the Reader is trawling frantically through his memory, '... only one who has resisted his temptations can stand against the Sleeker, best to avoid the Sleeker if you can, best to escape being put to the test ... ' he calls out.

The Keeper's holding firm in the Trifolium, his eyes on the glass, admiring the strength of the boy. The temptation is merciless. He can hear the unctuous voice ...*I only want the whistle. Throw it to me and I shall leave you alone.*

They watch the unequal battle, all the time circling the table while the Finder sings.

The boy is amazing, courageously holding out against such overwhelming power.

Under the Finder's singing they can hear the insistent persuasiveness. *Give it to me, Alex, you don't need it anymore.*

They watch in dismay as the boy begins to yield, starting to lift his hand from the whistle towards the thong, from the hard horn to the soft leather.

The Finder is singing strongly, but he cannot drown out the hypnotic quality of the Sleeker's command, *Give it to me, Alex, you do not need it anymore. Give it to me, Alex, you do not need it anymore. Give ....*

The inevitable surrender is coming. They can only watch, their hope draining away. Alex is beginning to lift the thong carefully over his head - then something stops him, he puts the whistle back, cradling it in his hand again.

The glass fills with blackness, hissing with heat, making them think it might explode.

Then it clears. They see The Sleeker towering in its rage over the boy.

The Keeper realises it's now or never. 'Grab hold of the fir tree! Do it now Alex!' he rasps.

The Sleeker, caught unawares, raises its sightless head and towers up, seeking this unseen enemy.

Alex reaches out desperately for the tree with his free arm and clings to it.

Now the Keeper urges, 'Blow the whistle, Alex!'

Alex clings to the tree, frozen, bracing himself.

Again the Keeper rasps, 'Blow the whistle, blow the whistle, Alex, blow it now!'

Alex looks puzzled. Then takes the whistle to his mouth and blows.

Enraged, the Sleeker locates them. The glass on the table blackens as it turns its fury upon them.

They hold out desperately, fighting back, warding it off while the Finder sings louder and louder …

There's a crash - their circle is broken - flinging them from the table. Down they fall, in a dark cloud of despair, down hopelessly, down, down, down on to the floor.

CHAPTER 18

Alex puts the whistle back over his head to think. The breath of scorching anger burns his neck, making him flinch.

Above him towers a menacing column of black, *You stupid boy! You cannot hope to resist me so now you shall pay for your disobedience*, a jet of stinking air hisses, hot in his face, making him cower.

'Grab hold of the fir tree, Alex!' comes a rasping voice he recognises.

The fir tree is close to him but his legs seem unable to move, 'Fight with your mind,' he tells himself. He thinks of Little Sal moving bravely along on her walking frame.

The black grip slackens. The Sleeker, distracted, searches for the enemy, the voice that's helping Alex, advising him to seek the protection of the tree.

Alex feels its powerful will depart. He stumbles against the tree, reaches out desperately with his free arm, seizes hold of a spiky branch, clinging on for dear life.

A vortex of hate screeches back over him. *You cannot hold out forever, boy! I can wait. I have you now ; you can never escape.*

The dark is closing in on him, clammy, he's very cold.

'Blow the whistle, Alex! Blow it now!'

Again, the black grip slackens.

Alex clings to the tree, motionless, bracing himself.

'Blow the whistle, blow the whistle, Alex, blow it now! ...' His Uncle Berwyn...?

Puzzled, he takes the whistle to his mouth and blows.

Fury explodes around him. The fir tree trembles, the earth under his feet shakes.

He's blowing the whistle strongly, hearing its silvery music.

The black hold on his mind lets go. He feels the huge presence moving away. Something else is engaging its fury.

At the same instance, a crimson and white light appears brightly down in the valley. It begins to move in great bounds towards him.

The whistle's music soothes as he blows. Huge surges of relief shake his body but he clasps the fir tree still, needing its power. The enemy has retreated, tears come to his eyes, blurring his vision in the dark world around him.

Suddenly, crimson and white lights flash from the trees below the moor. From its colours glowing just as the old legends say, he knows the creature bounding towards him, out of the dark, is a hound of Arawn. In a flood of joy he stops his whistling to cheer, 'The Hound of Arawn comes! He runs!'

One thing that none of the old myths had mentioned, but which is singular about the approaching hound, is the collar it wears. Strange! Luminous! Magnificent!

All of a sudden Alex realises it's Gobaith speeding up the mountainside. He watches, mesmerised by the sparks of light from the collar. They are like the coloured flames of a blinding Catherine wheel.

Gobaith arrives at the fir tree. He sits attentively in front of Alex, ears pricked, but he's unnatural, a huge hound; their eyes are level!

Alex realises Gob's waiting for him. 'What should he do now?' He looks around for inspiration but all he can see is the sparkling hound and the faintly glowing branches of the fir tree. 'Why am I here?' he asks himself in a daze.

The attentive hound sits patiently watching him, watching and waiting. The collar around its neck is pulsating, allowing the flow of a warm light.

Suddenly, Alex understands: the collar radiates love - pure love. It's a collar of love! He tries the question again, 'Why am I here?'

This time the answer comes at once, 'The ancient stone, Jack's carved stone, the stone of Aenlic Angharad!'

The hound senses the change and stands up, ready.

'Fetch!' he commands. 'Fetch the stone! Fetch it!'

Immediately, with its nose to the ground and tail wagging, the hound sets off searching round and about. It suddenly goes into a frenzy as the scent becomes stronger. Then stops and begins scratching at the ground with its paws.

Alex goes over to the hound and sees it's scratching at a large boulder. He squats beside it, takes the boulder in both hands and heaves. It does not move but then he begins to rock it with all his weight, suddenly lifting it, turning it right over. Magically, merry laughter fills his dark world; tiny bubbles, all of silver, fill the air. They slowly clear and an angelic face is looking up at him from the ground. The beautiful face fills him with noble thoughts, making him vow to right wrongs, to make the world a better place for the life he leads.

The face is shining, translucent, he longs to pick it up. He knows this is Jack's stone; he should take it, it's Jack's. But how can he... how can he, a grubby boy, dare touch something so pure? He stands with his head bowed, longing to hold this silver stone, but cannot do so, just for himself.

CHAPTER 19

When Sasha comes to, she's sitting on the ground. Nonnie's beside her holding her gently.

'Easy now,' Nonnie says softly.

'Where am I? What happened?' Sash asks, looking bewildered.

'You fainted, that's all,' Nonnie reassures her.

'Arrh! I wemember now,' she lisps childishly as she looks around in haste, 'Gobaith?'

'He's run off, with all that barbed wire round his neck, poor thing. He suddenly sprang up and bounded away,' Nonnie says looking west in the direction of the moor. Then she adds, 'There was nothing we could do. That's when you fainted, it was one shock too many, I suppose.'

'Where is he?' Sasha asks in alarm.

'He raced across the fields, down towards the river,' Nonnie answers. 'He went bananas, it was like he sensed something and was answering a call - he just went for it - he's gone all the way to the moor, I think.'

'But he can't get far with that wire round his neck,' Sash despairs, 'he must be losing loads of blood.'

The girls struggle to their feet and look across the fields towards the river and beyond to the moor. Gobaith is nowhere to be seen.

Nonnie glances at the iron bar near the fence. A length of barbed wire hangs limply from it. Patches of blood mark the ground, she sneers to herself, 'And I'd just been telling Sash how well those Vaughan boys look after their crippled dad!'

The door of the farmhouse closes, shutting Gareth off from the trouble he's caused.

They look round when the man with the first aid box says, 'Look, I'm Michael, Michael George. I'm staying at the Lion, just outside Tal-y-Cafn, for a few days' holiday. Let me help you?'

'You've done that,' Sash says, glancing at her bandaged hand.

Mr. George is calm and speaks with quiet authority, taking control. 'If your dog's gone all the way to the moor, it's going to need help.'

'Yeah, you're right,' Sash agrees.

'Why doesn't one of you go home in case he returns? I'll drive the other one up to the moor and we can look for it there.'

It seems like a good plan. They glance at each other a moment and back at Mr. George who's nodding in agreement.

Nonnie takes charge for a moment, 'Sash you've just fainted so you'd better go in the car, and I'll run home. I expect Mum's there by now, anyway. We'll wait, but If Gob comes we'll drive up to the moor.'

The sky continues to blacken. A storm is brewing in the mountains, perhaps the thunder storm of last night is circling back.

'Okay with me, Nonnie, do you know where to meet us?'

'Mr George, do you know the moor at all?' Nonnie asks.

'Actually I do,' he replies, 'my uncle used to take me caravaning in those hills, when I was a boy. We'll drive up to the Meirion Arms, we could meet you there.'

'Okay, that's a good idea, you've been kind, thanks,' Nonnie says and hurries off along the road to Gorswen shouting, 'See you later, Sash!'

As the car reverses, Sash catches sight of Nonnie moving quickly along the road. Then the car turns and Michael George moves through the gears, swinging the car sharply left-handed away from the farm. Her head rolls with the movement of the car onto her bandaged hand giving her a whiff of antiseptic mingled with aftershave.

The clouds are oppressive but Sasha finds the wind refreshing as it blows on her face in the open-topped car. She pushes her feet down onto the floor and stretches. The moulded leather seats embrace her comfortably and the car's powerful engine throbs reassuringly.

They drive up through a wood of oak and birch. Sasha finds the green of the trees soothing against the livid sky.

Michael George brings the gear stick down into second as he slows for the cattle grid ahead and the back of his hand brushes against Sasha's leg.

'Sorry,' she says in a hushed voice, moving the offending leg out of range.

The driver's eyes are fixed in concentration on the road ahead. He doesn't appear to have noticed the brief contact and the MG Sports rattles over the grid and up into the mountains.

As they climb higher, Sash notices the trees have changed, they are now driving through pine woods, Douglas firs and Norwegian spruce. She can also see a little stream, patiently winding its way down towards the valley they've just left.

Then the car spurts clear of the trees and into a world of rough grass, rushes and peaty, rock strewn soil.

In the middle distance, Sash can see a cluster of Scotch

firs surrounding a quaint building, covered in whitewash, the Meirion Arms.

There are only two cars in the ample parking area outside the inn. Clearly the lowering clouds are not attracting many tourists today. Michael George parks, flashing Sasha a smile, 'Right, here we are.' Then he points, 'Do you see that track over there?'

Sash looks. Gobaith is nowhere to be seen, however.

'It leads directly up to the moor. Why don't we go along it a short way so you can call for your dog and see if he comes?'

'Okay,' Sash agrees, zipping up her coat.

Michael George slides out of the car and goes to open the boot. He puts on a brown, leather jacket and fits a black and white checked cap over his hair. Then he takes some tarpaulin covers from the floor of the boot, closes it lightly, and begins to clip the covers onto the car, 'Just in case,' he says, glancing up at the threatening sky.

Sasha smiles nervously.

They cross the road and pass a new telephone box, which looks somewhat out-of-place in the remote surroundings.

Michael George leads Sash up the twisting path following a dry stream bed. The dark line of heather is visible above them, but as they weave their way up into the mountain they become hidden from view in the deep cleft.

Sasha's hand is throbbing and she hopes the climb ahead isn't going to be too steep.

CHAPTER 20

Heavy droplets of water begin to fall on Alex's head drenching his shoulders. The hound at his feet continues to glow, undimmed, while the face on the ground in front of Gobaith lifts Alex with its sweetness. Water cascades from the sky; washing the stench of the filthy assailant from the mountainside - but the threatening presence comes again like a bad dream.

Alex, horrified, knows: 'It's back!'

An angry fork of light, followed by a massive crash throws him into a lightless place. It's like an empty cinema. The projector light behind him starts up. On the screen, he sees a desolate moor. The camera zooms through a cleft in the rocks, panning from side to side zooming in on the faces of jagged rock. Moving lower now, it finds the path below. Sasha's face appears in close up. She's bleeding; she's gagged!

A lightning fork, a thunder clash erupt almost together. He's still in the airy room with the projector running. Now he's back with Sash in her terrace home. His arm is over her shoulder and there's a photo album on their knees.

'This one's of me being presented to the Prime Minister,' she's saying, giggling shyly.

He's looking at the photo; it's black and white. It clearly reveals the small girl on the left to be a younger Sasha. Her hair is tied in neat plaits; she is shaking hands with a dark suited man, who's clenching a pipe in his mouth.

The scene in front changes and he can see the on off, on off, on off, yellow lights of a pedestrian crossing. Sasha's walking down a deserted high street, where shop windows are lit with colourful displays. The dark, wet surface of the road is reflecting the rays of the street lights as the rain falls. He's holding Sasha's hand. It's good to hold, soft and warm. She stops, pulling him around to look at a pink pill box hat in the window - he can hear her laughter rising above the splash of the rain.

Suddenly his hand comes free from hers and brushes her arm. He feels a cord, rough cord? Sash is bound tightly!

We have her, boy, a voice jeers. *She's my slave; wrapped in my darkness. I've already shown you where she is. You know the place; you must bring me the whistle and the stone. Bring them to me at once.*

Alex comes to. He's lying on the dark mountainside. The ethereal hound is standing at his head licking his face, its tongue rough on his skin. The fir tree nearby gives a faint glimmer of light. He shakes himself. 'Oh, Sasha! Sasha! Sasha!' he yells in anguish.

Then he reaches for the stone to pick it up. He rolls forward, pushing himself to his feet, ready to leave the mountainside.

CHAPTER 21

Gavin notices the buzzard flying above them. He keeps his eyes on it because it's circling right over Alex, who's stopped in his tracks, just above the fir tree, he's standing rigid.

Gav feels Alex's stare pass straight through him, showing no recognition of him or the dogs. He can see the whites of Alex's knuckles around the whistle he's gripping furiously.

The sky is darkening by the moment, making the atmosphere sombre, more oppressive.

Gav senses something isn't right. He sees the hackles rise on Spray's back showing her wariness. The other dogs look cowed; they slink in behind his legs.

Alex is slowly taking the whistle up over his head but then he stops, anguished, before wrenching it back, clenching onto it again with his knuckled hand.

The lightning's going to strike at any moment. The air smells of sulphur; there's a metallic taste in Gavin's mouth. He looks at the fir tree, taking in the two blasted stumps beside it. 'Lightning has struck here before,' he notes grimly.

Alex is gasping for air. He's having a catatonic fit of some sort.

Gav goes over to him, catches his arm shouting, 'You okay?'

Alex doesn't answer. He doesn't even seem to see him or feel his touch.

Gavin stands there, frightened.

Suddenly, Alex stumbles away, lurching towards the fir tree. He's like a swimmer in a wild sea reaching out desperately for the life raft.

Gav looks in amazement at his cousin clinging to the tree with his right arm, clenching the whistle in his left. It's horribly weird. Gav reaches down to stroke the back of Spray's head for reassurance.

Strangely, Alex has the whistle in his mouth. He seems to be blowing it with all his strength but no sound's coming from it. He makes a disturbing figure, clinging to the fir tree with one arm, blowing a soundless whistle - it's like a nightmare.

The dogs huddle closer to Gavin. Spray is growling, there's something here she's warning off, or trying to at least.

Much to his surprise, Gav sees Gobaith bounding up to them. He's racing up at incredible speed. 'What's that around his neck?' Gav asks himself. Then a second later the answer shrieks back inside his head, 'Barbed wire!'

As Gob bounds up to Alex, Gavin notices the wire around his neck is drawing blood, staining his white fur.

He watches in disbelief as Alex springs into life and begins to work Gobaith over the stones. He urges him to hunt but, although Gavin can see Alex's mouth moving, no sounds come from it. Gobaith appears to understand, he's hunting the stone strewn slope energetically.

Then Gob stops. He begins scratching at something, pawing the ground in front..

Gavin sees Alex squatting down beside his dog. He's heaving at a large boulder that doesn't budge. Gav hurries over to add his weight to the heave when Alex rocks his body back in a huge effort. Now the boulder shifts, it turns over away from its resting place and there, lying on the ground before their eyes, is Jack's ancient stone.

Alex still seems unaware of Gavin. He stands over the stone, bends towards it but doesn't pick it up.

Thunder booms right overhead. In an instant a strike of forked lightning jags into the ground, driving Gavin and the dogs away down the hill. He shakes his head to clear it, 'That was close!' he shudders to himself. He looks up the hill. There's Alex. He hasn't moved. He and Gob are together. Alex is still bending over the place where the stone lies.

Lightning again zigzags down beside Alex; the crash of thunder roars. This time Alex is on the ground.

Gavin races back up the hill to help his cousin. The heavy rain begins to pour down, as he climbs the short distance.

He can see Gobaith licking Alex's face.

Just as he's reaching Alex, his cousin sits, picking up the stone face on the ground beside him. He doesn't appear to see Gavin or hear his worried questions, 'What's the matter? What's wrong? Are you okay, Alex?'

Instead of answering him, Alex leaps up. Without so much as a glance at Gav, he begins to stride across the moor, Gobaith at his side.

Gav and the dogs follow but, for once in his life, he can't keep up. Alex is marching away, his eyes fixed on the horizon, while the space between the cousins widens with every step.

CHAPTER 22

The stone in Alex's hand emits a silver light as he walks. It fills the air around strangely with sounds: singing, neighing, horses running. To his right, constant as a shadow but gleaming crimson and white, trots the massive hound.

Alex casts a backward glance at the fir tree, his recent refuge, which is glowing bravely in the dark. All around him is a black sea of heather. He is aware of a sinister noise in the void encircling him, an incessant hiss, buzzing louder at random making him duck away, a constant annoyance, disorientating - interfering with the natural sounds coming from the stone in his hand.

The heather gives way to rushes, tall, spiky against his skin. The ground is soft, it's insecure, at any moment he might push through the crust to the muddy bog beneath. He falters, it's then he hears the hated voice, *Come on boy, I won't wait much longer.*

The clammy hand of fear clutches his heart. It pulls him down to the cold bog-water of hopelessness. 'You must resist,' he urges himself.

The buzzing just outside his small pocket of light is louder, stronger, hate-filled.

He struggles on, coming to a large, flat rock lying among the rushes. It's covered in a thick growth of lichen, it's like snow in the silvery light of the stone.

Leave the stone and whistle here, if you choose, boy, the hateful voice suggests, *then you can rest.*

He shakes his head; the buzzing clears for a moment but then returns, louder, nastier than ever. He raises the stone closer to his ear to ward the hissing sound away. Now he hears the sound of approaching ponies, the wild ponies of the Carneddau.

Splashing through the rushes they come, a small herd of mares, fillies and colts but no stallions. He has seen these ponies often in his ramblings on the moor and only once spotted a stallion - they usually graze aloof on higher ground.

He steps up onto the lichen. The rich smell of ponies fills the air. The gigantic hound beside him turns to look at them, its tail wagging faster and faster like an accelerating piston.

The ponies sweep up to him and stop. A mare and her colt stand alongside his rocky platform. She rolls her gentle eye at him. Then gives a whinny. The natural sound helps dampen the bizarre buzzing.

Her colt squeezes itself in between Alex's rock and his dam. His coat is a silvery white, his tail a long, silver thread. He rubs his head along his mother's neck, lowers his head and waits beside her.

Alex understands they have come to help him. He releases his grip on the whistle, flexing the fingers of his left hand now they are free, easing their stiffness from the stress of clenching the bone so hard. Then he leans forward, throws his left leg over the colt and grasps its mane with his fingers.

He hears a hiss in his ear but this time it is a little less confident, it carries a note of exasperation. Then the angry buzzing resumes.

Away they go, through the rushes and up on to the heather clad ground beyond. The ponies seem to know where they're going. Alex holds the silver stone high in his right hand; beside the brave colt strides the loyal hound.

They arrive at the edge of the moor. Now the colt begins its descent, sure footed but slow in is his action, careful.

Alex finds himself sliding forward onto the colt's neck as the young pony steps gingerly on the steep, uneven ground. There is little for Alex to hold, his right hand is occupied by the stone but the colt is patient, carrying him well.

They reach the bottom of their downward climb and Alex pushes himself back a little away from his pony's head.

The herd turns left into a cleft in the rocky hillside. They move forward but, as they do, the hackles of the hound begin to rise.

Icy fear stops Alex's body, making him snatch for breath in frightened gasps.

The colt shivers, leaning in close to its dam. The herd closes in tight, there's a stamping of hooves as it does so.

Ahead, close to the sheer rock of the mountainside, towers something huge but too dark to see. Alex can feel its power, a force he felt on the mountainside way beyond his strength. It can bend his will, snap him in two like a mere twig, enslave him.

Its stench stings his nostrils; its malevolence cows his spirit.

The colt's ears flatten. Even the gigantic hound looks subdued. The stone in Alex's hand continues to emit its silver light but the dark tower engulfs Alex in black despair. The natural sounds from the stone are harder to discern, becoming drowned out in the strident buzzing.

What kept you, boy? comes the jeering voice from above.

CHAPTER 23

Sasha stops. She cups her hands around her mouth calling, 'Gobaith! Gobaith! Come on, good boy!'

Her cries bounce off the sheer rock faces, echoing along the twisting path. There's no sign of Gobaith.

She's feeling cross. Her hand's throbbing, the clouds are weighing down, she's broken a rule coming here alone with this unknown man. Also this enclosed, hidden space, doesn't seem the best place to look for their lost dog.

Michael George waits for her to come up to him, 'There's a likely place just up round that corner,' he says.

Sash is reluctant to come too close to him, she's aware of her isolation in this lonely valley with this man she doesn't know.

Sensing her anxiety Michael George does his best to reassure her, 'If he isn't there we'll have to go back to the car and wait for the others.'

'Okay.'

She walks on but, as she does so, there's a blinding flash, then a frightening clash of thunder just above them. She crouches down beside a huge boulder for shelter where Michael George moves right beside her.

'Storm must be overhead, you all right?'

'Yeah,' she answers. A second jagged fork strikes from above followed at once by the clash of clouds.

Michael George takes a sudden intake of breath. His eyes writhe, then his hand is clamping over Sash's mouth.

She shakes her head free of his grip, her shrieks bounce back from the surrounding rock.

He grabs her again, his fingers squeezing her mouth shut. 'What's he doing? He smells wrong, acrid, stinking, foul ... he's hurting my mouth!'

His grip is steel.

She tries to bite him but his hold is too forceful. Her jaws ache.

Her mouth's forced open, a large wad of cloth is pushed in - she gags!

He's tying something, it's hard around her mouth and head. She feels it cutting into the corners of her mouth. It really hurts.

She's about to choke.

She can't swallow at all, cannot feel her tongue. The filthy smell is making her dizzy, hopelessness is filling her mind with morbid thoughts - she wants to give up, simply surrender to the darkness enveloping her.

Her attacker seizes her wrist, spinning her round twisting it savagely.

He pushes her down onto her knees, an ugly, bulbous vein distorts his forehead. His mouth is wet with saliva, his wild eyes are full of hate. He ties her wrists together behind her back, before throwing her over onto her stomach.

She feels a knee in the small of her back, hurting her, it's pinning her to the ground. Terror stalks her, strong cord is being tied round her ankles. It's burning her skin.

She cannot separate her feet or hands; she's lying face down on the rocky floor of the cleft, thinking, 'Why did I trust this man?

How often was I told, "Never get into a car with a stranger."'

He rolls her over onto her back, sits her up, then drags her against the rock face so that she's looking down the path towards the Meirion Arms. Her knuckles squash against the back pockets of her jeans; her palms press against the cold stone;

Then he's off her. He's different – changed, she senses the alteration.

Surprisingly, he lies down beside her on his back. He lets out a mixture between a groan and a wail. He is lying next to her on the rocky ground, rigid, unmoving except for shallow, quick breaths.

The stench is worse than ever.

Sasha realises something really horrible is waiting there. It was present in the man beside her, rising up from where he lay, but it was massive. It's still there, filling the entire place.

The rain begins to fall, washing out of the sky.

The hopelessness remains; the stink's in the air, all around her, rank, everywhere - but the rain is pure, it's clean, it helps her.

She begins searching in her mind, looking for a thread.

The massive thing beside them is cunning but cowardly, This she senses. Daring, with a boldness that surprises her, she begins to approach it in her mind, unseen.

She sees a boy, a teenage boy, who is looking longingly at a fruit machine. *Just give it a try,* says a persuasive voice.

She watches as he puts his money into the slot and loses once, twice, thrice, then a win and then more losses until his money's all gone...

Now the boy is back again but looking shabbier. He is holding a purse in his hand.

He hesitates.

You can easily pay your mother back when you win, breathes the tempter.

He plays again, betting again and again until the purse is empty.

She feels its supercilious gloating, *A boy hooked, a family ruined.*

The can of worms is open.

She sees a lonely girl, shy but in company. They are passing something around for money, something illicit.

Go on, urges the slimy voice, *it will make you cool, lift you high.*

The girl hesitates.

Go on, what harm can it do? comes the silky question.

She gives her money and pops the pill. She's one of the group now, free of her loneliness.

Told you, didn't I?

Now Sash sees the girl again, thinner, looking dirty, uncared for. She'll do anything for her next fix, all she can think about is getting more of the drug she craves ...

Again Sash feels the supercilious gloating, *An addict now enslaved to her habit.*

This thing beside her, it's a destroyer, swollen in size with power from its victims, it's an enslaver, a filthy thing, a parasite.

The Sleeker, towering above her, has its attention elsewhere but as she stumbles on the truth, it's aware of her there. It had dismissed her as a puny girl, underestimated her.

Now it's stripped of its cloak revealing its empty pride.

Sasha, comes the oily voice, *I could give you what you really want*

...

Before it can tempt her any further, some mountain ponies come into view. In their midst walks a gigantic hound, its fur is glowing crimson and white.

Beside it, riding on a colt, is a boy. He's holding a hand up, high above his head. He's carrying a round object, a light of some sort that's casting a silver glow around them.

'Alex and the Hound of Arawn!' she thinks excitedly.

There's a hiss above her; the stench of sulphur thickens in the air.

CHAPTER 24

Gavin keeps his eyes on his cousin, striding across the heather into the wind, cutting his way through driving rain. Gobaith is ever present by Alex's side, a rain-soaked creature with a bloodstained coat from the coil of barbed wire wrapped around his neck.

After struggling to keep up, Gav stops tracking them through the thick heather. He moves up to the Drovers' Way, gaining the protection of the stone wall at its side. He watches his cousin's progress, across the hillside below, from there.

He can see Alex is walking awkwardly, his right hand in the air, marching through the heather. They are a strange sight, Alex and Gob.

Gavin bends low into the elements and trudges along the historic way with the four dogs as company. He's soon at the Chapel-in-the-Moor and stops to shelter at the well, just inside the stone wall. The famed holy well of St Trillo. He looks at its unruffled surface, the water is still, safe - a place of calm in the storm, steadying him for a moment.

He looks down at Alex, noting with dismay his cousin has veered away from the chapel, down into boggy, rush-covered ground. He can see Alex has stopped in the middle of the rushes. He watches him climb onto a long, granite slab lying there, Gob is still with him. He realises in horror it's the Judgement Stone. The place where an accused witch, in the old days, was brought to be tested. A barbaric place!

'He's gone wrong. Does he know what he's doing?' Gavin wonders.

He's about to shout when he sees the ponies. It's a small herd, about sixteen in number. A few mares and their off-spring, he notices, but no stallions, which is to be expected. To his surprise they enter the rushes to surround Alex and Gob. One of the mares goes alongside Alex on his rock. Then its foal, a pretty colt, pushes in as well.

'What's happening now?' he asks himself.

He sees Alex mount the colt, all the time holding his right hand with the stone high above his head, almost like a lantern in a dark cave.

Now the mountain ponies are on the move again, this time with Alex and Gob in their midst. They begin to climb out of the rushes, back to the purple moor.

The rain continues to fall, the wind is strengthening from the north west.

Gavin leaves the chapel, the well an unblinking eye watches him moving as quickly as he can into the wind. Soon he passes the sanctuary stone, standing stark, alone in the open country. He has no hope of keeping up with Alex and the ponies but can see them ahead.

'Maa! Maa!' It's a cry of distress but puzzling - no animal's to be seen.

Gavin stops, looking across the heather. It seems empty but he knows the animal is there, somewhere. He waits, listening.

'Maa! Maa!' the cry sounds close.

He steps off the way to search, parting the heather carefully, his dogs at his heels.

'Maa! Maa!' from below to his right.

He turns towards it, treading softly. He shifts the heather - there before him is a fully grown ewe. It's stranded in a peat bog, hidden by the heather. The animal cannot move.

Gavin edges round behind it. He puts his arms around its neck, leans back and pulls. At first it doesn't give, then there's a great sucking sound as it comes free of the squelchy peat.

Its front feet are on dry ground but its hind quarters are stuck fast in the peat bog. Its big eyes roll at him, 'An old lady this one,' he thinks to himself, 'a real old grandma.'

Gav moves to the front to help her. He stands astride her shoulders and grasps the wool on her back and heaves, heaves, heaves! 'Here you go, old lady,' he says softly as she struggles free.

She stands still, cold, stiff and shaken, to get her bearings. Then she begins to stagger down through the heather to find the rest of her flock.

There's no sign of the bog that held her captive. The heather has closed over it, concealing it from view. Yet the danger's real enough, a trap for the unwary hidden in open sight, deadly beneath the harmless heather, one mis-step and you're in, caught!

Gavin rubs his hands on his jeans, then he turns to climb back to the Drovers' Way. Once he's on the track, he looks towards Alex and the ponies but cannot see them. They are out of view, it seems.

He scans the horizon again. There! On the far edge of the moor he sees a small group against the dark skyline. 'That must be them,' he decides.

He calls the dogs forward, hurrying in the direction of the group.

They will soon be out of sight but he doesn't know where they are going.

CHAPTER 25

Nonnie hurries along the road to Gorswen, stopping a moment to look back on hearing Sasha being driven away in the open-topped car.

There's a storm coming.

She worries for Gobaith, then wonders how Alex and Gavin are getting on. 'Has Gob run to find them?' she asks herself. 'P'raps he's waiting for me back at home?'

She follows the road, twisting down and round into the yard at Gorswen. Her mother's car is not there; neither is Gobaith. She feels rather flat, 'What can I do now?' she questions herself in frustration.

She'd not expected to find them both at home but had hoped one of them would be at least. The place seems strangely empty, it's just a little eerie.

She gives a half-hearted call, 'Gob! Gobaith, here boy!'

Once inside she runs through her options. There's no point in her phoning Mrs. Griffiths the Post, 'Surely Mum won't still be there? Aled Thomas did say to call him if Gob wasn't found but we did find him, didn't we?'

She paces the kitchen thinking. Then she makes a decision, picks up the phone and dials. She hears Agnes Thomas answer.

'It's me Nonnie Lewis, can I speak to the Reverend Thomas?' she asks, speaking quickly but clearly.

'I'm afraid he's out, my dear.' There's a short pause before Agnes asks, 'Did you find your dog, then?'

'Yes but he ran off towards the moor.'

'Run off again.'

Nonnie can hear the disapproval in Agnes's voice.

'Mr George has taken Sasha in his car to find him,' Nonnie explains.

'Has he now? Kind of him, that should be all right then my dear, I expect.'

'Yes, I think so,' Nonnie agrees.

'Aled did say you could phone him at Tirion Mawr, if you need him, but as Mr George is helping, you won't need to bother him.'

'Yes,' Nonnie answers.

'I'll tell Aled you phoned when he comes back, my dear.'

'Thanks.'

Nonnie replaces the receiver, feeling slightly reassured. She picks up a magazine, sits down and flips through it, looking more than reading.

The sound of wheels outside, followed by a 'Toot-toot te toot-toot,' has her leaping to her feet.

Her Mum's flashing eyes and quick smile raise her spirits, 'Hurry Nonnie, there's loads of shopping in the boot and it's going to pour any moment now,' Enid says looking up to the sky. She's out of the car in a moment, ladened with bags.

As they pass, Nonnie says, 'I'll bring the rest.'

'Wait 'til you see how much there is!' her Mum exclaims cheerfully.

They've just brought all the shopping in when a fork of light jags high in the sky, followed by the crash of clouds, 'That was close,' Enid says.

The sky is livid. Another streak of lightning crisscrosses down to the ground then a clap of thunder reverberates loudly. Now the rain begins to fall in long lines from high in the sky. The heavy drops are bouncing off the car, exploding continuously all over the yard.

Pleased to have all the shopping put away, Enid makes them both a cup of tea. 'Where are the others?' she asks.

Nonnie unburdens herself readily. She has had a bit of a wait on her own, her anxiety has been rising even though she's normally quite unflappable and self-confident. She reaches the end of her account saying, 'So you see we decided to split up. I came home to wait for you,' she pauses, glancing up at her mother for a moment before adding, 'and Mr. George, who knows the mountains - he used to camp there as a boy, you know - drove Sash up to the moor.'

'All the way to the moor!' Enid's tone rises in surprise. 'Why did he need to drive so far?'

'It's just that Gob ran off in that direction so Mr. George offered to help,' Nonnie explains. 'I phoned Agnes Thomas and she said it'd be okay.'

'Did she, now?' Enid thinks for a moment. 'Well, I'm not so easy with this. Sasha's in my care, I promised her mum I'd look after her - now she's on her own with a man I don't know in a thunderstorm.'

'Oh Mum, there's nothing to worry about. He's nice. He's friends with Aled and Agnes. Besides, he's only gone to the Meirion Arms,' Nonnie says with a shrug of her shoulders.

'Well, I hope you're right,' Enid responds, zipping up her jerkin with a frown. 'Let's finish our tea and drive there straightaway.'

CHAPTER 26

Sasha fixes her gaze on the group below, which is lit by a light in Alex's raised hand. The light's silver, similar to moonlight but local . A number of ponies are packed around Alex. The gigantic hound stands looking steadfastly in her direction. The most striking thing of all has to be the collar the hound is wearing, it's pulsating warm rays towards her, they're blood-red, giving her hope as they beat.

The jeering voice, coming from above her, shatters everything, *What kept you boy?* it sneers.

She can see Alex. His head is turned in her direction. Then he sees her; his cry follows echoing off the rock faces all around, 'Sash-a! Sash-a!'

Just give me the whistle, hand me the stone, fetch the collar here. You can free her! the cruel voice cuts back.

She watches Alex dismount. He begins to move towards her, the stone light held high above his head. The boy with the light, the dog with the pulsating collar advance together. Hound and boy reeled in by The Sleeker's power. 'Surely they aren't just going to surrender?' she asks herself in consternation, sensing deep down that's exactly what's happening.

The whistle first, boy, the command's cold.

Alex is only yards from her now; she watches him stop. He begins to lift the leather thong of the whistle over his head. His action is awkward, it's a one-handed movement. He's holding the light giving stone in his other hand, precious light in the dark.

Sasha holds her breath.

Now the whistle is free in Alex's hand.

Give it to me here, boy, comes the chilling voice.

Alex holds the beautiful whistle, crafted from animal horn, into the darkness.

Easy to do, wasn't it boy?

When Alex brings his arm back into the pool of silver she's saddened to see the whistle has gone.

Now, I shall blow it correctly, the callous voice goads them.

Sasha hears an annoying buzzing repeating and repeating in her ears but - it's the action of the hound she really notices!

The hound begins shaking its head and body as though it's trying to clear water from its coat. It is shaking all over; its luminous fur is dimming. Now it is scratching its ears first with one paw, then with another. The poor creature's in pain. It begins to circle round and round and round, suddenly it's crumpling at Alex's feet curling into a tight ball. Worst of all the collar around its neck begins to pulse luridly green, a sickening light sucking hope away.

Give me the stone next, comes the ice-confident command.

Sasha feels black hopelessness descend. She knows Alex will obey. He holds the stone, his hand is clenched around it, moving it down and away.

The silver light vanishes; the buzzing increases in intensity hurting her ears, deafening in the darkness. At the feet of the dark form she knows is Alex, pulses the green light from the collar. It is mirthless, cruel, aching her body with cold.

I must have the collar now, something sadistic in the voice really frightens her.

'How can the collar be taken without killing the dog?' she wonders, horrified.

In its cruelty, its greed to gain power over them all, the Sleeker has made an error, an oversight. Its attention has been fixed on Alex, the hound and the objects of secret power - these it must possess - but it has failed to discern the Searcher right alongside, a dangerous opponent: one who can see into and find, a seeker after truth.

Sasha realises now, any second the collar's going to be ripped cruelly away! Help ... she must help the hound ... she has to find a way at once. She looks out into the darkness.

Sasha's grasping for it with her mind, 'Blackness and a green light?' At that instant her finger explores the pocket of her jeans, there's something there. It's smooth, shaped like a small comb but softer, gentle on the fingertip. With her wrists tied tightly together, she cannot do more than just touch it. 'What can it be?' Of course, it's the raven feather, the one that floated down from the sky! The one she'd caught and pocketed.

There! Deep in her subconscious Little Sal's dream diary flicks open before her: shows her raven down ... black ... feathery; the green-eyed raven ... beautifully embroidered, 'Bran!' she thinks in recognition - the lid of darkness, leaden, heavy upon her, shifts and lifts.

High above, a raven's croaking.

Huge raven wings are clearing the clouds: light is streaming in, golden beams of light are coming from behind a lamb on the high mountain. Someone's running towards her, a young woman whirling something shiny above her head. In a flash Sasha knows! It's Sal, strangely transformed: stronger, wiser, older. She's like a beautiful prophetess. Sal's racing bravely, hurrying to save them from beyond the grave. As she runs she's wielding her walking frame above her head, sprinting along the golden track of light, an arrow of hope shot from the sun.

Sasha's gag is tight, sore, pinching the corners of her mouth, the linen pad hard against her tongue … yet she's laughing, seeing her sister coming so fast!

Water pours down the rock; rushing away in torrents.

The massive presence beside her sways, hisses. Caught in the open, it falters.

Sal is upon it, whirling her walking frame like a shiny sword, 'Back you must go! You tempted me once, remember? I resisted … refused your deceitful offers, remember? Arawn was there, licking my hand. I chose the other way, remember?

Now I have the right to face you, to send you back to lightlessness where you must remain … you seek to ruin, to despoil, to enslave all who live in light … you cannot stay.' Sal's whirling the walking frame like a windmill blade as she speaks, shredding the black tower into pieces. 'I pity you. I know you could have chosen another way altogether. This I know … I feel so sad at the choice you have made, at the choice you keep making. You ensnared yourself long ago, your craving for power makes you its slave, you must depart!' Pieces of the tower form into a black pool at her feet, it slides into the torrent taking it away, away, back to its lightless morass, hissing, frothing down from the mountain.

The clouds continue to clear. The summer sun bursts through making Sasha blink, for a moment she cannot see and when she does … Sal's gone.

Alex rushes forward. His hands are on the knot at the back of her head, releasing the gag. He pulls the linen pad away, throwing it onto the ground..

Sash sucks in the air. She works her tongue across the sore edges of her lips, moving her aching jaws.

Alex works quickly at the knotted cord around her wrists.

She feels the tension in it slacken and slips one hand out, free.

Alex pulls the cords off the other hand.

Sash rubs her hands over her wrists which are stiff and swollen. She wiggles her fingers and flexes her thumbs allowing the blood to flow in and heal.

Alex is down at her feet. The knot is loosening, then he's unwinding the cord - she's free. He moves beside her, putting an arm around her shoulder.

On the ground, just below Michael George's feet they can see the whistle and Jack's ancient stone, lying together.

They say nothing, just rest in the moment, exhausted.

A sudden movement makes them look at Michael George. He's holding his arms crossed over his chest, rocking to and fro. His eyes open, wild, crazed. Then he croaks, 'It's gone! It's left me! I really am free, free, free!' He stops rocking, lies there still, looking up into the blue sky hugging himself.

They understand. They have felt its presence too; they know something of the black hopelessness it casts.

Michael George turns to Sasha, 'Sorry, so sorry,' his voice breaking.

Sasha nods. She tries to smile but her lips are too sore so she grimaces at him.

Michael George gets to his feet. He moves to Gobaith who's lying beside Alex.

Gob lets him come.

He takes some pliers from his pocket, shiny, new like all his kit. He gently prizes the blade around the wire … snips, again he snips … again until all the barbed wire is free.

It is something he can do. They understand this.

Gobaith licks his hand.

Michael George checks the ruff of fur, congealed with blood around Gob's neck. There are lesions, very many small cuts but no huge gash.

They sit there in the sunshine without speaking. Alex and Sasha together, with Michael George next to Gobaith who licks his new friend's hand.

CHAPTER 27

The Keeper rouses himself. He has been woken by a raven croaking in his ears, a flapping of wings vibrating in the air - on his lips the word, 'Bran!'

The Reader stirs with the raven sound as well, he's thinking of Bran, the son of the sea god, Llŷr, and close friend to Aenlic Angharad in the old days ....

The Finder is pulling them to their feet, saying, 'Buddies, how those raven feathers ushered in the light in my head, awesome man!'

Now they regroup around the Abergwyngregyn Eye. The Finder resumes his holy incantation as they join hands and circle round it, their attention fixed on its bubbly blue-green glass.

The Finder's strong voice rings out:

'There is a balm in Gilead
To make the wounded whole
There is a balm in Gilead
To heal the sin-sick soul ...'

and as the bubbles begin to clear the glass fills with golden light.

Then the Meirion Arms swings into focus and they see Michael George's MG Sports parked there. The next instant the winding path up into the rocky cleft is shown and grazing, quietly in the shelter of the hollow, are a mare and her colt and other mountain ponies - they make a peaceful scene.

Round and round the Trifolium circle slowly with their hands joined and their gaze fixed on the glass.

Now they can see Sash and Alex sitting with their backs against the sheer rock. Alex has his arm around Sasha who's resting her head against his shoulder.

The watchers of the eye do not stop their actions, then the glass gives them another insight. It shows them how Michael George is sitting just below Alex's feet next to Gobaith. They can see Gobaith licking his hand. Between Gobaith and Michael George are heaped cuttings of rusty barbed wire, speckled with dried blood.

Then the golden light fills the glass once more, a moment later it resumes its normal state of trapped bubbles in a blue-green glass world.

They unclasp their hands coming to a stop.

'Well,' the Keeper rasps, 'I think we'd better drive up to the Meirion Arms at once.'

'Indeed, we must,' the Reader answers.

'You go straight away then. I'll put this back and follow you,' the Keeper rasps, 'I'll need my Land Rover for the dogs.'

Within minutes, Jack and Aled are driving into the car park of the Meirion Arms. Jack draws up beside the MG Sports and turns off his engine,'That didn't take long, bud,' he says.

'Indeed not, my friend,' Aled answers.

They climb out of the car and, as they close its doors, they hear another car approaching, 'Gee, Berwyn wasted no time,' Jack says. He turns to look at the approaching vehicle but is surprised to see a Ford Escort, instead of the expected Land Rover, pulling in and driving over to them.

Enid parks. She and Nonnie leave their car to join Aled and Jack.

'Have you seen Sasha and Mr. George?' Enid asks, looking at Aled.

Before he can answer, the sound of another vehicle catches their attention. They turn to see Berwyn's Land Rover entering the car park. He drives over to the group and unwinds his window.

'Enid here's looking for Sasha and Mr. George,' Aled says quickly.

'And we're here for Gavin, Alex and my dogs, they've been caught in the storm,' Berwyn explains.

Gavin strains forward into the driving rain. Alex, Gobaith and the ponies are out of sight, and he realises that he must cross to the edge of the moor because he might see from there where they've gone.

The moor is a plateau on top. While the mountain ponies traversed it with relative ease it's more difficult for Gavin on foot. The heather is thick, waist high in places, and there are several wet patches where he sinks into the peat. He is fit and quick but it takes him some time before he is near the edge of the mountain.

When he is about a quarter of a mile from the end of his march, the rain slackens and the wind drops. Then the black clouds part and a rainbow, radiant with arcs of coloured light, appears in all its glory right in front of him. Out through the arc of light swoops a raven, its dark wings glistening as it glides easily, freely in front of Gavin.

His spirits soar, jumping into a run, with the dogs alongside him, he's off - hurling himself towards the magical light. Arriving at the far edge of the moor, panting to catch his breath, Gav scans the country for his cousin, Gobaith and the ponies. His legs are aching, the blood's thumping in his neck but he's wildly excited.

Expectantly looking down the hillside, mapping the ground in a one hundred and eighty degree half circle - Gav sees nothing. The ground's wet, water's cascading along rivulets, peaty brown, frothing white in patches. The black clouds are receding rapidly and the welcome summer sun is warm on his back, making steam rise up off the heather and gorse.

He looks again more carefully. His pulse is calmer now. Away to his left and far below are some boulders, strewn over the ground. 'No they're not,' he tells himself, 'they're ponies, mountain ponies blending naturally with the landscape. I bet Alex and Gob are near them.'

Gavin walks along the hilltop in their direction and when he is level with the ponies he begins his descent. It is easy to start with but it soon becomes steeper and he has to move cautiously over the slippery surface. Soon he is reduced to creeping down on all fours. Then he comes to a sheer drop - pauses to catch his breath - one slip here will be fatal. He lies flat on his stomach and cranes his neck forward. In the hollow below he can see a gathering of people and a dog - it must be Gobaith, surely?

He inches his way back from the edge and sits up. Below to his right a few sheep are feeding, steadily grazing, moving slowly in search of new shoots. Now he can see a sheep track winding its way down to the cleft, 'That's the way to go,' he directs himself.

The dogs run ahead to herald his arrival. They bound at speed, tails wagging, to greet Berwyn and company. Some minutes later, Gavin is down on the winding path and greeting Alex, Sash, Nonnie and everyone.

CHAPTER 28

Gavin, Sash and Alex are squashed into the back of the Ford Escort, Nonnie's in the front with Gob at her feet. Enid's following the MG Sports. Michael George is driving down into the valley with Aled as his passenger and guide. They're going to the Chapel-in-the- Moor and its healing well of St. Trillo just above Garnedd Wen, The White Cairn.

'Couldn't keep up with me today, Gavin,' Alex is teasing.

'Well, I didn't ride a horse, had to use my own transport, didn't I?'

'A horse? As if!' Alex exclaims with mock indignation.

'I saw you on that little white colt!' Gavin remonstrates.

'And how'd I find a tame pony to ride up there or do you think I just climbed on to a wild one?' Alex laughs.

Sasha and Nonnie are giggling too, as the car crosses the Gyffin and begins to climb back up to the high ground of the Eryri Mountains.

The road widens, then the cars line up behind the MG. Berwyn leaves his dogs in the Land Rover, opening all four windows for ventilation. The air's fresh after the rainfall, the soft light of an August evening is on the wall lining the path, still warm in the sunshine. Alex strokes the horn of his whistle, remembering how Gobaith had answered its call so bravely. Jack follows just behind him, in the pocket of his jacket he can feel the weight of the stone face Alex has returned to him.

Aled leads the way up to the chapel. It's a steep climb and he pauses to catch his breath. 'Haven't been here since Christmas carols,' he says to those below, 'quaint but freezing, it was! Fitting for "In the Bleak Midwinter" of course.' Then he turns, taking the narrow path up to the door of the chapel.

They don't enter the chapel but follow Aled round to the Drovers' Way on the wild side of the building. He finds a wrought iron gate built skilfully into the stone, opens it and steps over the threshold into the burial ground surrounding the little chapel.

Aled leads them to the far corner where the ground drops away a little and there, nestled between the walls and lined with local slate, is the well, the healing well of St. Trillo.

Aled calls Alex and Gobaith forward.

Alex takes off his hiking boots, he sits with his bare legs dangling in the water of the well. The water is cold. It soothes his tired feet and feels good. Gob lies beside him resting his head on his lap. Alex cups his hand so the water fills his palm. Then he gently sprinkles it over Gob's neck wounds, once, twice and once again.

Sasha joins them, swishing her feet in the healing waters. The cool water washes the grazes made by the cord, soon she's leaning forward to bathe her sore wrists, allowing the water to ease the rope burns. She splashes water onto her face and lips, feeling cleaner, fresher, liberated.

Finally, Michael George lies face down beside her and dips his head under the water, once, twice, and once again.

Sash hears a voice in her head, the voice of her sister Sal, 'Forgiveness is the balm of all.'

There is no balm as such to hand but she understands. As Michael George sits up, she cups her hand in the water and sprinkles its contents gently first on his right hand and then on his left.

No one moves or speaks. The warm light falls upon the three of them and on Gobaith too, turning the water of the well to gold.

Aled comes over, takes Michael's hand, pulls him up onto his feet and they begin to make their way back to the gate.

Gavin looks out over the wall across the moor. He can see the rush-covered ground below, where Alex and Gob had veered during the storm, the large rock is empty. He smiles as he remembers his cousin climbing onto the white colt - 'As if!' he chuckles. Then he turns to join Nonnie on the path.

Berwyn and Enid are in quiet conversation as they leave the burial ground, their heads close together in a brother and sister catch up.

Jack comes forward and kneels beside Sasha. 'Hey,' he says confidentially to her and Alex, 'this blessed carving wasn't safe in my place buddies.' As he speaks, he takes the ancient stone from his pocket and places it into Sasha's hand.

She runs her fingers over the carved lines, caressing it, recalling the silver light it brought them in their need.

Alex too recalls the beauty of the light and the sweetness of its melody.

'Hey bud, place it face down on the floor of the well for me, will you? It's the safest, best hiding place I can think of for now.'

Sash looks at him to make sure he means it and sees he does. She turns over onto her tummy and reaches down into the well, gently placing the ancient relic face down on the slate strewn floor.

As she does so the water fills with bubbles of light drawing her into the world of the well. The bubbles clear and she can see a large pool of water, held in a massive scallop shell. Water is bubbling into the shell from above and as she looks up, she sees it is flowing out from the mouth of a mermaid statue. Sitting beside the shell is Sal, smiling happily, stroking a dog, that's very like Gob.

Now Sal, seeing Sash, waves brightly. Then she points. There's something she wants Sash to see.

Sash follows her finger to the foot of the statue, noticing an old water jar made of limestone. It has an inscription and she can just make out the letters, *kalal*, on its side. To her surprise, a raven swoops down, lands on the rim of the pool and looks at her with - green eyes!

Glancing at Sal, she receives a thumbs up sign.

Then the light in the well darkens. Sasha continues to stare down through the water to the various stones on its floor. She wonders if Jack and Alex saw … but it's time to rejoin the rest of the group.

Leaving, she takes a last look at the well, its water steady, calm, peaceful, watching her go like the open eye of the Earth itself.

CHAPTER 29

'Hello … Gloria? Yes, it's Enid Lewis speaking … Yes, that's right.'

There's a pause before Enid continues, 'I just thought I should give you an update.'

Enid listens at some length.

'Sash is fine but I wanted to let you know that she hurt her hand; I've checked it … yes I have … yes that's right … it's a bit bruised but nothing's broken. I've put a dressing on it as she has a few cuts. I'll keep an eye on it so no need for you to worry.'

Enid listens once more.

'No trouble at all, Gloria, I'm glad to help. Yes, I'll call her now she's just in the kitchen, hold on.'

Enid puts the receiver on the chair beside the phone and pops into the kitchen, 'Sasha I've got your Mum on the phone, I've told her about your hand, and she wants a word.'

'Or two,' Alex adds with a cheeky grin at Sash.

The kitchen's cosy. Gavin and Nonnie are sprawled on the sofa; Alex on the old settle beside the fireplace. Cups of tea and buttered Welsh cakes are on the table.

Sash gets up from her seat to take the phone, 'Hi Mum,' she says quietly.

Then she listens with the phone in her right hand. She shakes her head slowly, raising her bandaged hand up to her chin.

'No, Mum, that won't be necessary, I'm okay, really, I am.'

She listens again.

'No Mum, Enid's checked it out already, she's going to put fresh dressings on it in the morning … I'm lucky to have my own private nurse here, aren't I?'

Her hand on the receiver tightens as she listens at length to her Mum who is speaking in her free-flowing way on the other end of the line.

'No honestly Mum, it isn't necessary, I'm fine.'

Her Mum's off again into another lengthy speech but this time Sasha is nodding her head.

'Yes, of course, I promise. See you on the 27th, oh and thanks Mum, love you.' Putting the receiver back, she smiles at Alex as if to say, 'You know what she's like.'

'Well, what did your Mum say?' Gavin asks from the sofa.

'Oh, she wanted to know if I was okay.'

Alex puts a reassuring arm over her shoulder.

'Did I want to go home?' Sash continues. 'Should she come and collect me, or would I be all right on the train? She worries a lot, always has really,' she adds sympathetically.

'What did you say, Sash?' Nonnie asks.

'I said I was fine … that your Mum was looking after my injured hand well. I just said I wanted to stay here as arranged, of course.'

'Good for you, Sash,' Nonnie says, throwing an arm around her.

'But then she suggested she could come and stay in a nearby hotel.'

Enid brings some more biscuits and sits down in the chair next to Nonnie's end of the sofa.

Sash looks at Alex, 'Dear old Mum, I don't know what good she thought that'd do,' and she starts to laugh.

Nonnie begins to laugh with her.

Sash is laughing louder as she continues, 'She was ready to start out straight away in our clapped out Mini!'

Now Alex is laughing helplessly, making a strange 'H-u-oop! H-u-oop!' as he sucks the air into his lungs.

They are laughing away as Enid looks on bemused, 'How quickly the young recover,' she thinks. Then she notices that Alex has a pat of butter and a bit of Welsh cake squashed onto the back of his jeans, now she's laughing with them, her auburn hair shaking joyously.

CHAPTER 30

Berwyn's sitting in his armchair lost in his thoughts. Open on his lap is a folder of his late wife's artwork and writings. He has taken to looking over these on evenings when he's not so busy.

His dogs are sprawled on the assortment of rugs around his chair, resting - the excitement on the moor lost in the steady rhythms of their breaths.

He's thinking of his lifelong friendship with Aled Thomas, his reading of the signs and wise scholarship ... the Whistle of Cambria, safe in his keeping once more and how he was right to entrust it to Alex. He feels a glow of admiration for the boy as he recalls how bravely Alex held the whistle and used it to summon help at the moment of crisis.

'The signs were there to see, of course,' he thinks. He recalls the time of his sister Ellen's separation and divorce. Sad days that had brought her and the boy to stay with Enid that Christmas, years ago, and how he'd given Alex the puppy, now called Gobaith.

Gobaith - who had been so magnificent today - the finder of the ancient stone, the bearer of the collar, the most faithful friend to them all!

Back his mind drifts to that Christmas - how Alex and his puppy had walked over to see him on Christmas Eve. Enid had sent over some mince pies with his nephew who'd stayed for the afternoon to play chess - played so well that they had been locked in battle for hours. He smiles at the memory as he revisits their surprise at the vast fall of snow, coming so quickly, and which they'd failed to notice in their focus on the chess pieces before them.

'Of course the roads were impassable,' he recalls with a smile, 'so a quick phone call to the girls and a promise that we'd walk over to Gorswen early on Christmas morning settled the matter.'

He'd made Alex and Gobaith comfortable in the box room and waited up for Christmas Day to begin. He remembers climbing the stairs with a small stocking of presents for Alex to open in the morning, placing it on his bed as the clock downstairs chimed its way to twelve o'clock.

'Ding- dong, ding-dong, ding-dong,' - three strikes, one quarter and the puppy on the floor began to glow faintly.

'Ding- dong, ding-dong, ding-dong,' - three strikes, two quarters, now the puppy on the floor was glimmering, pulsating a gentle light from its coat.

'Ding- dong, ding-dong, ding-dong,' - three strikes, three quarters, and the puppy was dazzling like a shooting star.

'Ding- dong, ding-dong, ding-dong,' - three strikes, four quarters, twelve midnight! How he'd stared amazed at the puppy's brown markings, its ears and part of its tail were glowing a rich crimson colour, the rest of its coat was gleaming white. 'A hound of Arawn,' he'd realised as he drew in his breath.

He relishes all of this, especially now.

In the months that followed he'd consulted regularly with his scholarly friend, Aled, and they had leafed excitedly through several manuscripts.

More recently, Jack had found the ancient stone carving; it was then they knew the time of trial had arrived.

He returns back to the events of the day, 'The girl, Sasha, must be so very strong in her mind, she's absolutely fearless too,' he feels a surge of admiration, thinking, 'despite her cords and gag, she managed to summon Bran when all seemed hopeless - such boldness, in one so young, to look into the darkness and see!'

He sits there making his plans. He'll spend tomorrow in his workshop, there's a lengthy inscription to chisel into the chosen slate.

Then he leans forward and looks down at the folder on his knees, turning the page. Now on the left there's a water colour of a farming scene opposite some verses on the right.

He glances over the writing. It's in his wife's elegant handwritten italics, and reads:

Mountain Shepherd

He calls you one by one
Listen, hear him whistle.

At the gate beyond
See it's there he stands.

Can you see him now
Waiting, crook in hand?

He will always lead.
Can you follow him?

His dogs will keep you straight
They listen to his words.

He whistles, whistles loud
Showing you the way.

Sheep are you behind?
Hurry sheep, can you now?

You may pass to grass
Safely go to pasture,
If he is your guide.

Watch for wolf and danger
Keep secure within the fold,
Little lambs, can you?

Choose the drover's way;
Keep him always in your sight -
Sheep and lambs, stay close.

Follow him over hill
If you will ... if you will ....

With this instruction still echoing in his mind, he looks over the watercolour on the facing page.

It depicts a mountain scene, showing a flock of sheep walking up between two stone walls towards an open gate. There's a shepherd, holding a crook in his hand, his back to the sheep looking ahead over the stone wall at the country beyond the gate. This is left to the imagination, because the stone wall screens it from view.

The dry walls on either side of the sheep are high and skilfully built.

One of the sheep, towards the back of the flock, has a tuft of wool on the top of its head that looks a little like a barrister's wig. He smiles wondering if his wife had someone in mind?

Below the flock, a sheep dog is busy keeping them moving towards the shepherd. An interesting detail is the dog's colouring, not the usual black and white but a more striking brown and white, a reddish brown and the white, glossy in the sunlight of the painting.

Some aspects of the scene remind Berwyn of their evening visit to the Chapel-in-the- Moor. The warm light is similar as are the stone walls, but that isn't all – there's something in the mood of the piece, it's really familiar!

He looks beyond the shepherd. All he can see on the other side of the wall is the sky, a cloudless blue, filled with stars.

The longer he looks the more stars he sees. It's obviously a sunny day but the sky is filled with stars - 'Thought provoking that.'

Berwyn leans back, his mind turns to Brutus, 'Why poison my good friend?' He has his suspicions of course but can't be sure, the question sits, unanswered.

Now he's back with the water colour. It looks like a simple farming scene, a shepherd and sheepdog moving the sheep to new pastures but there's that otherworld quality? He notices a pine is growing out of the stone wall on the other side of the open gate from where the shepherd stands. The tree's the size of a mini-Christmas tree but now as he looks closely, he sees its strangeness. The half on the side of the approaching sheep is green, a rich dark green with a hint of blue, but - and it may be just a trick of the light - the far side of the tree seems to be aflame!

Then - the gateposts. They are carefully crafted from the stone, and are clearly strong but the bottom half of each post looks odd, rounded, bulbous. He examines them closely and realises that built into the bottom of the posts are two large stone jars, and neatly inscribed, so he can just read them, are the letters *kalal* carefully crafted on each one.

'That's not a word I know. I must remember to ask Aled.'

There are so many questions in his head as he sits there thinking but the most persistent is, 'Why poison Brutus, why did they need to poison my noble friend?'

CHAPTER 31

There! There it is again!

Scratch, scratch, scratch! The sound of a paw scraping the wood on his bedroom door.

Ever since he buried Brutus, Berwyn's nights have been disturbed by this visitor.

He climbs out of bed and opens the door but there's nothing to be seen. He examines the door for scratch marks. None! He returns to bed, lying there, intrigued.

Berwyn thinks of the legend of Arawn and his hounds. They seem real but are not of this world; they cast no shadows in the light of the moon.

He knows the story well with its ideas of friendship, keeping your word above all, living with truth - proving your worth when tested. His mind fills with bright images of the ethereal king ... his magical hounds lighting a dark landscape as they run together in their pack ... their baying echoing in his head ... slowly he drifts off, away from consciousness.

Scratch, scratch, scratch! The sound of the paw against his bedroom door again. He switches on the light, but there's nothing there. He looks down, expecting the door to be untouched.

Clear marks are scored into the varnish, marks he's not seen before....

Finding a slipper, he places it between the jamb and the door, fixing it open. 'If it wants to come into my room, it may do so now,' he reasons.

He slips back into bed, falling into a half conscious doze filled with dreams running one into another. He dreams of a lady on horseback. She rides past him at a modest pace, her face is veiled. He's curious so he springs up on his horse, expecting to catch up with her easily. His horse bounds away at speed but no matter how fast he rides the lady always remains a distance ahead of him.

She rides past a boy playing with dogs in the snow. His attention is drawn to them, and he realises it's Alex, a much younger Alex who's holding a tennis ball high above his head, two dogs are watching intently. He can see one of the dogs is no more than a puppy, 'Oh it's little Gobaith!' he exclaims to himself.

Alex throws the ball high into the sky. It lands with a thud, disappearing into the snow. The dogs keep their positions, sitting at Alex's feet, they're both looking eagerly in the direction of the submerged ball.

'Brutus, fetch it! Fetch it, Brutus!' comes Alex's high-pitched command.

The bigger dog, which has similar brown and white markings to little Gobaith, begins to hunt for the ball. It searches with its nose in the snow, travelling in wider and wider circles from Alex and Gobaith, its tail wagging excitedly as it works. Berwyn knows it's his dear friend. He watches with pleasure as Brutus finds the ball, then brings it back to Alex, dropping it at his feet.

The ball is picked up and thrown again. Alex sends Brutus to fetch it once more and he begins a second search.

A cloud clears from the moon overhead. Berwyn can see the mountains ringing the horizon to his right, on his left he's able to make out the orchard fence and a mound of newly dug earth. The lady on horseback has stopped her horse there and turned so she's looking back down at Alex and the dogs. Her face is still veiled; she's silver, in the reflected glitter of the snow.

Alex throws the ball again but only a short distance and it lands with a plop. Both dogs are sitting and looking in the direction it was thrown.

'Gobaith, fetch it! Fetch it, Gobaith!' Alex urges his puppy.

The puppy begins to hunt, circling round just like Brutus had done. Its small tail is pumping with excitement. Then it stops, plunges its head into the snow and comes up with the ball and begins to dance towards Alex, shaking snow from its ears as it goes.

Berwyn laughs. He wakes up with a start, but laughter is in his heart. Then words begin to run rhythmically in his head:

'A good dog, a true dog, running home.
A hard task, a long fight, safely won.

Bounding …
Panting …

… through wild night skies

At scent of danger …

A good dog, a true dog, waits for you.'

In the morning, he wakes refreshed but the question of Brutus is lying there at the back of his mind …

He thinks he knows why Brutus was poisoned - at last the penny's dropped. He rises from his bed to look once more at the door. Yes, the scratch marks in the varnished wood are plain to see, it's as he expected.

Later that morning a blue transit van with the words:

Roberts and Roberts
Slate/Llechi
Blaenau Ffestiniog

emblazoned on it rattles up to the house. It sets the dogs off barking and brings Berwyn to the back door.

Owain Roberts unwinds his window and asks, 'Do you want it put in your workshop?'

'Yes, great,' Berwyn replies.

Owain manoeuvres the van alongside the workshop so the back doors open almost into it. Then he and his brother, Trefor, manhandle the long piece of slate inside, placing it where he directs.

'So you're still keeping your taid's and your dad's old trade going then?' Trefor Roberts observes.

'Once mastered, never forgotten,' Berwyn answers. 'It's good to give their old tools an outing now and then, I'll give mine a rest and use theirs on this job.'

'That's top-quality Blaenau slate as you ordered. I'm sure you'll do a tidy job with it,' Owain grins, stepping into his van. The twinkle in his bright eyes turns serious as he adds, 'Sorry to hear about your dog.'

'Thanks boys,' Berwyn rasps as they turn their van around.

'See you then!' Owain calls above the sound of the engine and the van rattles off on its way.

Rolling up his sleeves, Berwyn enters his workshop. The room's cool, dark - but the slate is in place. He places his palm, flat on its surface, his fingers explore the stone while the rhythm, a running rhythm plays in his ear:

A good dog, a true dog, running home…
By my Master's side I race and roam;
Through the wild night skies…

At scent of danger -
Bounding above the bracken clad hill …

A good dog
A true dog …
Waits

CHAPTER 32

Alex and Sasha have Gorswen all to themselves because the Lewis family have gone to the dentist. They're enjoying the freedom - just the two of them and Gobaith, who's sprawled on the comfy rug in front of the stove.

Alex is staring into Sash's blue eyes. Her iris is rich, dark with flecks of light - the pupil at the centre is black, round, impenetrable but behind it she's looking out at him, inviting him in, holding his attention, keeping him spellbound.

Their hands meet. Their fingertips touch; their eyes locked pupil to pupil.

He feels the edge of her nails, sharp against his skin. His hand moves on to her arm, holding it gently above her wrist, avoiding her injured fingers.

She searches his eyes, her look is deep, beautiful, enchanting.

He cups his free hand around the back of her head; their lips meet.

She opens her mouth, letting his tongue in. She finds the back pocket of his jeans with her hand, slips it inside, pulling him into her.

Her hair is smooth under his palm.

Their lips widen, working in unison, as their bodies press together.

The hand in his pocket tells him what he already knows, he'll do anything for her. She's warm against him. He couldn't speak if he wanted to but there are no words for his feelings anyway. He's just so happy because she is Sasha, always.

Gob's bark interrupts them. A car's stopping outside the kitchen door.

Sasha tidies her hair with her bandaged hand, then turns to see who's just arrived. Out of the window, she sees Aled Thomas taking a hefty package from the boot of his car.

Alex throws the door open saying, 'Bore da, Aled. Have you come to see Enid? I'm afraid she's out this morning but come on in.'

Aled comes into the kitchen and plumps the heavy parcel on the table,'It's the two of you I've come to see.'

'Take a seat, Aled, tea or coffee? We must look after the postman,' Alex says laughing happily at his own little joke.

'Coffee, diolch.'

'How about you Sash?'

'Tea for me, Alex.'

In no time they are seated at the table with Sasha and Alex on the high-backed settle and Aled Thomas in the chair beside them.

'Well, Michael George is staying with us for a few days now,' Aled explains. 'He's with Agnes as we speak, organising that chapel carpet she's set her heart on - very generous of him I must say. There's no shortage of money with him, you know. I've heard he's giving old Vaughan a new wheelchair, an expensive one too - part of a deal that was struck which he intends to honour, so he says.'

'Is he really?' Sasha asks.

'Yes, he's been to arrange it and placed an order as well.'

'How is he?' Alex asks before adding, 'Must 've been shaken up.'

'Seems to have made a remarkable recovery, I think the healing water of St. Trillo has something to do with that - just look at your Gobaith!'

'Oh, yes, he's a picture of health. Aren't you Gob?' Alex says ruffling his dog behind the ear in the place he likes.

'The only thing is Michael George intends to report himself to the constabulary for his assault on you, Sasha,' Aled Thomas confides, suddenly serious and looking Sasha in the eye.

She holds his look.

He's aware of her extraordinary strength, her power of mind. It makes him think, 'It was this youngster who managed somehow to summon Bran at the moment of crisis.'

'Tell him,' she says,'I do not want him to do that.'

Aled watches her, listening intently.

'Tell him my Mum's easily worried, she only knows I've hurt my hand and that's how it needs to stay.' She pauses, 'Mum thinks she looks after me but it's the other way around really!'

She holds his eye, she has more to say, her blue eyes shine with sincerity. 'Tell him, also, I saw our assailant. I know it wasn't him. Tell Michael that, will you?' Her eyes show her determination, her soft voice, adamant, tough as diamond.

Aled gives a slight nod of his head to show his agreement, to acknowledge that he'll do as she wishes.

She continues, 'Tell him I understand something of what he must have suffered. I feel for him.'

'Indeed, Sasha, I'll tell him all you say, I assure you I will,' Aled replies, smiling his approval.

She drops her voice speaking in a whisper so that they can barely hear her. 'Tell him, also … it began to tempt me, promising me what I really want.'

Aled nods sympathetically.

Her whispers continue, 'I know I couldn't have resisted for long but luckily for me Alex arrived on his pony - there in the darkness I saw the Hound of Arawn beside Alex with the stone of Aenlic Angharad held high, shining its silver light - imagine it - I was on the precipice about to fall ... It's unthinkable! Their love pulled me back from the horror, saved me from the web of its sick promises, from its sticky temptations beginning to hold me fast - yech!'

Alex is looking at her with empathy, his admiration glowing. He's shaking, remembering how she saved him when his will was overpowered. He shudders as he recalls something of his surrender of the whistle, the giving up of the shining stone and of preparing himself for the savage ripping of the collar... nausea sickens him ... ugh!

Sash is still holding Aled with her eyes. 'Perhaps, Aled, you'll tell him some of that too as much as you judge to be wise?'

'I'll tell him how you felt the power of the tempter too and say how you understand the very great difficulty of resisting something so strongly malevolent,' Aled replies. Then he adds, 'Of course, you're right Sasha, he should leave things be. And I'll tell him so.'

'What's in the parcel?' Alex asks, changing the subject to something less serious.

'Well,' Aled replies,'it's from Michael for Sasha. He's finished his studies, done very well too I understand, but is now joining his father's business, international shipping, so he's got no further use for these, and would Sasha be interested?' pushing the heavy package across to her.

She opens it deftly.

It holds lots of folders, some are bulky and some slim.

Each one is carefully labelled in black ink.
The first two she looks at are:

'The Chronicle of Cynewulf and Cyneheard;
The Voyages of Ohthere and Wulfstan.'

She slides them across to Alex before picking up the rest of the bundle, reading out their titles as best she can:

'The Wanderer,
The Seafarer,
Aelfric's Homilies,
Kalal and Amphorae,
Runic Inscriptions
Ancrene Wisse'

'Wow, that's a lot!' Alex exclaims.

'Indeed it is,' Aled agrees, 'mostly Anglo Saxon I see.'

'What does kalal mean?' Sash shoots at him.

Aled's surprised by the speed of her question, 'Well that's Aramaic, it refers to the large waterpots that were used for ritual washing - long before the Anglo Saxons, that one,' he adds.

Aled turns to Alex and hands him an envelope, 'This is for your uncle could you give it to him? It's from Michael George as well.'

'No probs,' Alex says, taking the envelope.

'Strangely, I saw Berwyn's car parked outside Carreg Arw as I drove over,' Aled comments, 'I thought about stopping but thought better of it - you know what the Vaughans are like.'

'Hmm, I wonder what he's doing at the Vaughan's place?' Alex muses, looking at both Sasha and Aled.

Aled rises to his feet saying, 'Well now, I'd better be going.'

They follow him to the door.

As Aled opens his car door he looks up and catches Sasha's eye.

She returns him that long look.

'Yes,' he says, ' I'll tell him what you said Sasha. Yes, and you're in the right too, indeed you are.'

CHAPTER 33

Sash and Alex arrive at Tirion Mawr in the early afternoon - they've left a note for the others on the kitchen table.

They're enjoying the warm sunshine but Gob's panting in the heat. Berwyn's dogs are lying in the sun but spring up barking as they approach. A farm vehicle's parked close to the back door where Berwyn's talking with a couple of men. One is Gareth Vaughan.

'Strange,' Alex exclaims under his breath to Sash, 'that's not his usual company!'

Gob's hackles rise, he begins growling, a deep rumbling, showing his unease. He's not forgotten the barbed wire!

Sash looks straight at Gareth. Her arms hang straight, they're down at her sides but her fingers have curled, involuntarily, into her palms making her knuckles whiten.

He stares back at her, takes in the bandaged fist then scowls at the ground. His face reddens before he looks back at her for a moment, just a glance, then away again.

She stands frozen; her eyes on him.

Berwyn's explaining, 'The Vaughan boys are giving me a helping hand, come and see.'

They follow him into the outbuilding.

A new piece of slate, recently engraved, stands by the door. On the top of it, like a sort of crown, pieces of barbed wire have been set into the stone. They've been spray painted gold before being mounted and look impressive.

It's the wire they'd cut from Gobaith's neck! Alex's hand instinctively finds Gob, to give him a comforting stroke.

The Vaughan boys pick up the heavy slate, heaving it between them behind Berwyn up through the garden to the orchard fence. The strain's evident on their faces as they carry it to the mound of newly dug earth. Here they slide the slate down ready for planting.

Berwyn holds out a spade, 'Use this.'

They watch Gareth struggle at the earth, a bead of sweat on his forehead. The ground's hard, dry. There's a scrape of iron on stone as he toils, digging slowly deeper into the tough earth. Gareth's red shirt is crimson with sweat.

Alex rolls up his sleeves.

Berwyn puts out an arm to stop Alex, 'Let him do it all,' he rasps.

Eventually Gareth hands the spade back to Berwyn who nods. The Vaughan boys begin to manhandle the slate, working it laboriously into place.

They heave it here, there, back a bit, straighten it, lower it, before Berwyn is satisfied, 'That will do.' Turning abruptly, he leads them down to the house.

Once they're back beside their truck, Gareth says defiantly, 'That's settled then?' as he and his brother climb in.

'The least you boys could do,' Berwyn answers.

Sash glowers at Gareth, 'How's your Meg, feeding well?'

Gareth looks annoyed, his temper's rising but the truck roars into life in reply as they drive off without another word.

Berwyn says, 'That's an end to it, then.' He turns to Alex and

Sasha, 'Well come on in. You timed your visit well, I must say.'

They follow him into a spacious kitchen. Pointing to a table in the window, Berwyn says, 'Take a seat. It's thirsty weather. Would you like a drink, I've some cans of Coke in the fridge?'

Alex glances at Sash before answering, 'Thanks , that'd be great.'

The sun's filtering across the table lighting the room cheerfully.

Their drinks are bubbly,refreshing. Alex takes a slurp before saying, 'Aled Thomas asked me to deliver this, it's from Michael George.'

Berwyn takes the envelope, opens it and reads through its contents. 'Well this doesn't entirely surprise me, I'd begun to guess you see.' He passes the letter over to them, 'Take a look.'

Sash and Alex lean over the letter:

Dear Berwyn Davies,

After talking matters over with your friend, Rev Aled Thomas, I have decided to write to you about your spaniel, Brutus.

You should know that, in my rooms in Aberystwyth, I made the mistake of my life. I take responsibility for this because it hinged on a choice, a free choice – my free choice. At the time I did not realise how serious this choice was but, of course, that is not an excuse. All I was interested in were the archaeological discoveries I was making. I was lured by the esteem I would be gaining for myself, the fame that would be mine, my ego egged me on … I was

intoxicated by thoughts of my own cleverness, blinded, so when the Sleeker came, offering me scholarly achievements, glories, I fell, easy prey, not brilliant but stupidly gullible .

The Sleeker entered me. I shudder to write it... It created hell inside me, then grew and grew, ruling me at will. These were desperate days. I had to do its bidding, but I suffered as it filled me with black despair. It was cruel, callous. I was its slave, my better nature hated its control of me, but - enough of my ordeal which was of my own making - this letter is about Brutus.

You may recall paying a visit to the Thomases this spring. You were giving your dogs a ramble in the countryside. On your walk you decided to drop in on your friends. I happened to be visiting, coming to see about the new carpet for the chapel, to thank Aled for the help he'd given me. However, I was really there at the command of my owner, the Sleeker, to steal Jack's ancient stone and obtain the Whistle of Cambria too, if I could.

Well, you went inside with Agnes and Aled, but my controller, The Sleeker, made me wait a moment outside. It wanted to scrutinise your dogs, using my eyes. I found myself looking at each dog in turn, staring at them, feeling the Sleeker's cold contempt congealing my heart. Now that is when the transformation happened. Your dog, Brutus, began to change before my eyes. Its ears glowed bright crimson and its coat gleamed.

The demon inside me shook. I could feel its fear, its repugnance and its malice. It hated this creature but was wary of it; I sensed its cowardice for the first time.

One thought dominated all others, *Destroy! Destroy! Destroy!*

Brutus had revealed himself.

The Sleeker enlisted others to its cause, through me, I am ashamed to write. The Vaughan brothers were promised what they wanted and like me became trapped. Gareth and I plotted the poisoning of Brutus and the stealing of Jack's ancient stone carving.

Enough said, I think, the important thing is that you know about your brave Brutus, and his opposition to the Enslaver. Brutus was a dog of courage, he lived up to his namesake, Brutus of Rome.

I detest the part I played in the destruction of your gallant dog. I cannot bring him back so will have to live with the consequences of his destruction with the distress it has caused you and others. I know nothing in my power can make amends.

I am free now. I am free to make my own choices again. I am free thanks to the bravery of your nephew and that of Sasha - free to make the right choices and to lead a good life.

A life, I hope, that will help to make our world a better place.

Yours sorrowfully,

Michael George

Sash looks up, open mouthed at Berwyn, 'I thought Gobaith was 'The Hound of Arawn' but now Brutus seems to be?'

'I made the same mistake,' Berwyn admits. 'I saw Gobaith transform when he was a puppy, years ago.' He looks at Alex, 'That Christmas in the snow, do you remember?'

'Yeah, how could I forget?' Alex asks rhetorically, relishing the memory. 'We played chess all afternoon just didn't notice the snow 'til it was too late - had to stay over on Christmas Eve.'

'Well, I stayed up after you went to bed, waiting for Christmas Day,' Berwyn explains, 'and as the clock downstairs chimed the quarters for twelve midnight I was placing a small stocking of presents at your feet. That's when I saw Gobaith glowing, his ears crimson, his coat a brilliant white - amazing - so I've known about Gobaith for years.' Berwyn pauses as he reminds himself of that time before adding, But I'd never thought Brutus might also be a Hound of Arawn… not until recently that is.'

'That's impossible really, isn't it? They can't both be the "Hound of Arawn" can they?' Sash asks.

Berwyn stands up saying, 'Come with me to the sitting room, I'll show you Aled's written piece on Arawn, based on his studies of "The Mabinogion."'

He begins searching in a corner cupboard, picking up a purple folder. They settle comfortably, Berwyn flicks through the papers until he finds the page, ' Here it is. Shall I read it to you?'

'Yes, thanks,' Alex says as he ruffles Gob's ear.

'Long ago, when nobles hunted for their food, Pwyll the Lord of Dyfed was riding to hounds in his forest. Whilst riding with his hounds he became separated from his companions and blew his hunting horn loudly, turning north, south, east and west as he did so.

Then to his great surprise he heard the baying of ghost-hounds coming towards him.

As the pack bounded into view he was astounded at how different to his own hounds they were. These were like none he had ever seen. Their coats were dazzling white, and their ears burned a crimson red.

Behind them rode a man whose eyes shone like the sun, he had a hunting horn slung around his neck and rode a huge, dapple-grey horse that glittered constantly like the stars. This rider reined-in his horse and said to Pwyll, "Lord I know who you are, but you know me not, I am King Arawn …"

Here Berwyn stops, 'Well that's enough isn't it?'

Always so quick on the uptake, Sash exclaims, 'So there's more than one Hound of Arawn! I see, Arawn has a whole pack!'

'Precisely,' Berwyn answers, 'both dogs were hounds of Arawn but I missed that, you know - never thought of it at all.'

'Don't see how you could've, really,' Alex says.

'No, but I'd just begun to suspect some of it, Berwyn replies, a hound has been disturbing my nights. Also, I've been dreaming of Brutus and Gobaith. Do you remember training Gobaith in the snow with Brutus?'

'Yeah - Gob learnt so fast and Brutus showed him how to fetch and how to stay,' Alex enthuses, smiling at the memory.

'Well, I've just been dreaming of that now after all this time, but there's more, come and see,' and he leads them upstairs to show them the scratch marks on his bedroom door.

'What do you make of these?'

Alex and Sasha take a look, 'Looks like something's been scratching it,' Alex answers.

'They look fresh to me,' Sasha comments after bending low to look closely.

Berwyn sees the puzzled look on their faces and explains, 'I'd been disturbed for nights by a dog scratching at my door but it left no sign, so I thought I'd been dreaming. Then the other night these marks appeared - so I've left my door open since - guessed then it must be something to do with Brutus.'

'Michael George's letter confirms your guesses then?' Alex suggests.

'More than!' Berwyn replies.

'Do you think Brutus used himself as some sort of decoy to shield Gobaith somehow?' Sasha asks suddenly.

Berwyn pauses, 'That's certainly a thought, hmm, don't see why not!' making it clear to Sash he thinks her suggestion is probably correct.

As they make their way back downstairs Sasha asks, 'Does the word kalal mean anything to you, Berwyn?'

'Strange, you should ask me! I'm intending to ask Aled about that very word, myself. You see, Nancy, my late wife painted a watercolour of a farming scene where that word appears twice.'

'Really?' Sasha asks, intrigued.

'Yes, and I only noticed it recently, would you like to see?'

'Oh, can I? '

'I'll get it for you now, before you go.'

Sash turns to Alex, 'A bit of a coincidence don't you think?'

'Sure is,' comes his answer.

Then Berwyn's back with the water colour. Sash takes it, 'Come over to the window Alex so we can take a good look at.'

Alex says, 'It's very like the Drovers' Way by the Chapel-in-the-Moor isn't it?'

'Yes - it does have a look of it, with the stone walls and the sheep on the move to new pasture.' She looks closely at the painting and starts, 'Wow, have you noticed those gateposts?'

'What about them?' Alex asks.

'Look at the lower parts, I mean the bulging bits at the base. Can you see the writing there?'

'Oh! I see what you mean, "kalal's" been written on each one,' Alex answers with sudden interest.

Berwyn comes over, 'What do you make of that?'

'Really interesting, she was a good artist - I wonder what she means by those gateposts with "kalal" inscribed on them? Could this be a message?'

She pauses, pondering, feeling the mysterious pull of the past, the weird magnetism of these old water pots.

'Follow your heart, Sasha, it'll show you the way,' Berwyn counsels, placing a reassuring hand on her shoulder as he joins them by the window.

Sash looks at the painting again but keeps her own counsel. She's remembering Little Sal pointing at that old jar. The one illuminated in the water of St.Trillo's, when she put Jack's stone to rest.

Still holding the painting, she looks up at Berwyn to ask, 'Those are unusual markings for a sheep dog. Aren't they normally black and white?'

'Yes, to answer your question, the reddish brown and white markings are less familiar, but you do see sheepdogs that colour now and then.

You're full of astute questions, Sasha,' Berwyn adds, 'no wonder the others told me The Searcher was here in our midst.'

'The Searcher, Uncle B, what do you mean?'

'I told you ages ago about the Trifolium, Alex.'

The serious tone in his uncle's voice stops his questions. He looks enquiringly at Berwyn knowing there's more to come.

' Well, we have long awaited this, knowing The Searcher would appear at a time of great trial,' Berwyn pauses again to organise his thoughts.

Not even a dog moves while the clock ticks loudly.

'Testing times are here are they not?'

'Ah! Yes, I see... it was Sash who sought Bran, she saved me and Gobaith just as we were being overwhelmed,' Alex looks at Sash, his eyes shining with new understanding.

She says nothing.

She knows she's always liked searching for things but this title, The Searcher, seems strange, making her a bit on edge, sensing grave responsibilities ahead, especially after what happened on the moor.

'Alex, do you notice anything about the sheep in the painting?' Berwyn asks.

Alex has a good look, 'Can't say I do,' he says with a shake of his head.

'Look at that sheep near the back,' Berwyn directs, pointing at the one he means, 'look at its head.'

Alex laughs, 'Oh, it appears to be wearing a barrister's wig, I see what you mean!'

'I expect Nancy was having a small joke,' Berwyn chuckles remembering her teasing and fun character.

'Well we'd better be getting back - or Enid might think something's happened to us,' Alex says, still grinning at Nancy's clever joke hidden in her painting.

'Yes, I look forward to seeing you this Thursday for our big bash before you head back to London,' Berwyn rasps, smiling at the two of them.

'Come on then, Searcher Sash!' Alex half teases, hiding the seriousness of his Uncle's new title for her with a smile.

CHAPTER 34

Alex and Sash come back into the kitchen after giving Gob his late-night walk. Gavin and Nonnie are already upstairs, but not yet asleep.

Enid is just about to turn in as well, 'Good night you two, we'll be late tomorrow night if I know anything about the hospitality at Tirion Mawr, so I'm turning in prompt.'

'I don't suppose we'll be far behind you,' Alex replies, 'sleep well.'

'Oh, I usually do,' Enid says with a yawn, 'all those health visits wear me out you know.'

Once they're alone, Sash puts Michael George's folder, marked "**Kalal**", on the table and they sit side by side on the high-backed settle to have a look.

The document is about thirty pages long but the second half is mainly photographs of old stone jars of various sizes, massive stone crosses and slabs of stones with runic inscriptions. There's also a photograph of a striking stone font with carved faces protruding from its sides like watchmen.

The early part of the document is handwritten. Alex says, 'That's Michael's italic writing, isn't it?'

Sash gathers the papers and taps them on the table bringing them neatly into a block putting it down at the first page. Their heads are close as they begin to read the notes.

KALAL

Epiphany!
- Short Cross, once Tall Cross, located at Two Gates, shows the way.
- Water from Dozmary Pool & stone from Rough Tor need to be brought to the church door.
- Check also: Sanctuary Cross, Halvana Cross, Occasiney Cross, Trekennik Cross, Tresmeak Cross & view St. Vincent's Mine Cross.
- St. Nonna – the key here, I deduce. In Wales, Dyfed, she is St. Non. So, the link to Arawn and Aenlic Angharad is surely St. Nonna???
- Go round by Treween, Trewent & Tredaule
- Take in Tregunnon & Tolborough too.
- Check Palmers Bridge & South Carne, & Bowithick
- Go to the valley of Penpont Water.
- Cathedral of the Moor, may hold the centre!!!.... still not convinced Kalal's there?
- It awaits The Searcher!

IMPORTANT... should help The Searcher:

The twelve are the days,
At the dark time
When most life dies,
The only days of the year
For success
And the twelfth is the best
The Epiphany?

'The Searcher, Sash, he means you, I think?' Alex says feeling both excitement and alarm as he wonders what Michael George means by, 'It awaits The Searcher!'

'Do you think he does?' she asks before adding, 'The Epiphany? That's when the Wise Men arrive after Christmas isn't it? I remember it from primary school. We performed a play about it.'

'Bet you were an angel, Sash,' Alex replies quietly.

She flashes him a smile.

'I wonder where these places are?' Alex questions. 'They seem a little like Welsh, for example Penpont Water might mean water at the end of the bridge.'

'Yeah, there seems to be a Welsh link, after all he mentions Dyfed, St Non, Angharad and Arawn doesn't he? Lots of places in Wales begin with tre too,' Sash agrees.

'You mean like Tregarron or Trelawnyd near us? Could almost belong with these place names, couldn't it?'

'Hey!' Sash says suddenly. 'When we stayed at Bolventor on Bodmin we visited a church that had a carved font like the one in that photograph,' while she's speaking, she flips the pages back to the photo of the font with the carved faces. She's excited, her heart racing.

Alex studies it, 'I've never seen a font like that,' he says, 'not that I'm an expert on fonts, baptismal or typescript for that,' he adds as an afterthought, chuckling.

'I remember it now! Dad was always looking at the stone crosses that holiday. I remember him telling me that palmer was an old word for pilgrim, it's because they would carry palms to the holy places they visited - he was explaining the name Palmersbridge, I think.'

'So you're suggesting these are places in Bodmin, Cornwall?' he asks.

'Yeah, I'm pretty well certain,' she says softly. The idea comes to her and it's out in a flash, 'How about Christmas in Bodmin? There's a lovely holiday cottage I know, it's not that pricey, I'm sure I could persuade Mum.'

'Sounds good, do they allow dogs?'

'I think so, Gob's got to come anyway because we're going to need him,' she answers, her blue eyes alight. 'Certainly we need a Hound of Arawn with us, a protector, a hunter, we must have both to pursue this thread drawing us South West, leading us to Cornwall and Bodmin Moor!'

Sasha has trouble getting to sleep after all the talk of Bodmin Moor, her plan of going there for Christmas with Alex and Gobaith, the mysterious Kalal …

Sleep is fitful, punctuated by a series of weird dreams. She dreams of her father:

He's out on the moor walking away from a stone cross.

A voice is shrieking after him, in pursuit, *Stop the Searcher! He must never find it!*

Then there are ponies, numbers of them running free, beautiful to see but they are suddenly swallowed by a dank mist blowing in from the coast.

It's dark, wet, freezing - she's back on the bridge below Clitheroe, the town where her father was born.

She's pulled her bike to the side of the road.

The horses come into view, glorious animals, their eyes golden in the dark of the night. They're drawing a carriage. Her dad's driving, he's waving at her, Sal's up alongside him. She puts her curled hands up to her eyes to look at Sash as if through binoculars.

'Searching? Oh, **The Searcher!**'

Sal takes her hands down to give Sash a thumbs up sign …

Now in her dream she sees a lady, her face veiled, riding her horse steadily away, away, away. The dapple-grey seems effortless as it moves, smooth and easy.

Alex is suddenly beside her, he has the horn whistle in his hand. He puts it to his mouth and blows.

The sweetest music fills her heart - hounds are bounding towards him, their ears glowing crimson, their coats gleaming, ghost hounds are coming, creatures of light, not of this world … ethereal.

CHAPTER 35

Scratch! Scratch! Scratch!

Berwyn had forgotten to leave his bedroom door ajar which means his sleep is disturbed again.

He clambers out of bed and throws his door open saying, 'Sorry old boy, I forgot.' He steps out into the corridor for a moment, looks and listens, then he hears a scampering sound from his bedroom.

He turns back towards his bed. Bathed in moonlight, there on the rug beside his bed, he can see what looks like a hound curled up tight. He tiptoes over so as not to disturb it, enraptured by its crimson ears, its dazzling coat, flickering like starlight.

He kneels down beside the hound. He can see it has a collar around its neck but, as he reaches to touch it, his hand passes right through coming to rest upon the wool rug.

The hound is roused. It raises its head, turning its gaze upon him, loving brown eyes.

The eyes of his faithful friend.

This time he can see the name tag hanging free from the hound's raised neck, 'Brutus.'

His eyes fill. A mist obscures his sight and he has to blink the droplets away. When he looks again there is no hound there, simply the soft rug silvered by the moonlight, just him kneeling next to it.

He knows it will be tomorrow night. The moon will be at its fullest. Alex, Gobaith and Sasha will be present, along with other guests. It's their last night before returning to London.

He lies in bed thinking about the preparations he's made. It's time to hand on the horn whistle, The Whistle of Cambria, to Alex. He will continue to be Keeper of the Abergwyngregyn Eye for a while longer but Alex will now keep the whistle, he's to be the next in a secret line of Keepers. Alex has shown his mettle.

Although this gift will be made when they are among friends, he has decided to hide its significance by giving presents to Gavin, Nonnie and Sasha as well.

For Sasha he has one of the limited copies of Aled Thomas's version of 'The Mabinogion,' beautifully illustrated and leather bound, a nice touch that - from the Reader to the Searcher via the Keeper.

He has bought Gavin a handcrafted barometer, set within a piece of Welsh slate from Blaenau Ffestiniog, and plans to tease him about reading the weather and not getting caught out in thunderstorms.

Nonnie's present is a book he has written himself, 'The Complete Guide to Puppy Management.' It's one of a limited edition and there's a whole chapter devoted to Labrador puppies he knows she'll love.

Always generous to a fault, he's enjoyed choosing these gifts. He's looking forward to surprising his young friends at the party

Despite his sadness for Brutus, he's in a buoyant mood as he gradually drifts off to sleep.

His morning alarm clock is the high, well tuned voice of his cousin Rhian, who has always helped him entertain since Nancy died. He lies in bed, watching the dust dance, it's bright in the sunlight warming his room. He listens as she sings:

"... while the blackbird was cheerfully singing,
I first met that dear one, the joy of my heart!
And near us for gladness the bluebells were ringing
Ah! then little thought I how soon we should part.

Still glows the bright sunshine o'er valley and mountain.
Still warbles the blackbird its note from the tree;
Still trembles the moonbeam on streamlet and fountain ..."

He sighs contentedly. Rhian has a sweet voice but the words of her song remind him of his own life experience, in particular the death of his dearest one, so he feels its melancholy.

Rhian's busy when he comes downstairs. She and Berwyn are planning to give their friends a real treat. There's a chocolate souffle to be made and a prawn cocktail starter to be prepared as well. The centrepiece of the meal is a huge turkey and locally made sausages with enough roast potatoes to keep even Gavin quiet for a bit. It's to be a Christmas Feast in August.

From Berwyn's point of view, the evening party has been a long time coming. Now at last the happy hubbub of conversation fills the house as his clock sounds the quarters for seven o'clock.

Woof! Woof! Woof! erupt the dogs as Poppy nearly knocks Sasha's drink from her hand.

'That'll do,' Berwyn rasps, 'back to your mat and sit!'

His dogs return to their places looking expectantly at the door.

Bu-ump! Bu-ump! And a final bu-ump! Car doors slamming shut.

'Berwyn, you didn't tell me there were going to be others here?' Enid questions him happily, breaking off her conversation with Rhian.

'Didn't I?'

'Jack!' Alex says enthusiastically, 'come on in.'

'One second bud, ladies first, after you Agnes,' and he stands back to usher his neighbour into the house.

Soon the noise of conversation has reached a higher level as jokes are told. Aled's jovial laugh's ever present as it lifts all the company to heights of merriment. He's always a good person to invite to a party!

What a jolly dinner it is too! The prawns are delicious, the turkey supreme and the chocolate pudding sensational. Jack entertains them with one hilarious story after another, each time provoking great, booming laughter from his friend, Aled, which spreads in waves of joy across the table. Alex's sides, taut within from food, ache as he laughs and laughs.

Berwyn's gifts come as a wonderful surprise. Gavin is delighted with the barometer despite all the teasing about hiking in thunderstorms.

'If the needle points to Stormy Gav, it means don't go up into the mountains, it means the sort of weather where I'll easily race you,' Alex laughs.

'You and your mountain ponies, you mean,' Gavin counters.

There's a hush when Sasha's given her copy of 'The Mabinogion.' Aled withdraws into himself, a little shy for once, although he's clearly moved by Berwyn's gift to her.

'I'm really pleased to get this to read,' Sasha beams, 'there's quite a bit here I need to catch up on, thank you so much,' and her blue eyes hold Berwyn in the depth of her sincerity.

'Well, Sasha, I must say I've been a bit creative with the facts, like those St. Dogmaels' monks, and have embroidered some of "The Mabinogion" with my own imaginings - so you might like to check my work against one that's more precise and true to the original,' Aled comments. Then he produces a cardboard cylinder, looking like it might hold a small telescope. 'This is for you, don't open it now. It's for a private moment later, if you have some time to kill,' he laughs.

When Nonnie receives her book, 'The Complete Guide to Puppy Management,' she's flushed with excitement, 'We'd better get a puppy now, Mum!' she exclaims to a burst of approving cheers.

Alex is astonished by his gift. Berwyn keeps his gaze momentarily as if to say, 'We know what we know about this don't we?'

Rhian's murmur is only just audible, 'It's old and very valuable I dare say. We don't have the craftsmen any more.'

Alex cradles the horn whistle in his hand, 'Thank you, I'll keep it safe, thank you Uncle Berwyn,' and he puts the leather thong over his head, allowing the whistle to hang there in its rustic simplicity.

Jack says, 'Gee, it's like Thanksgiving today, turkey and presents. Hey buddies, let's play a game!'

Nonnie and Gavin leap up together saying, 'We'll organise Monopoly, Agnes will you do the bank as usual?' And they rush off without waiting for her answer.

By unspoken agreement everyone's moving off to the Monopoly in the living room. Sasha and Agnes are at the back together.

Agnes glances furtively at Sash, producing a small, silver tube, not bigger than a pen and gives it to her, 'I'd like you to have this,' her voice softer than usual, 'it's a torch and it's real silver.'

'Oh, wow, thank you, that's so kind,' Sasha says, taking the gift in surprise.

Agnes's small fingers press Sasha's hand a moment and she says, 'Don't tell the others, will you?'

'Not if you don't want me to, I promise.'

'Yes, good,' Agnes nods, looking pleased.

Soon the game of Monopoly is in full flow. Agnes manages the bank with quick precision making the game rattle along. With so many players it's not long before some are bankrupt. Sasha, Alex and Berwyn are among the early losers forced to leave the board.

Jack proves to be a shrewd player, he soon takes control of all the stations as he lands on Fenchurch Street, 'Gee I'll buy that too, Agnes, now all the railroad is mine and boy will it cost travellers some dimes to take a locomotive,' he chortles gleefully.

The clock chimes.

Gavin's building houses on Euston and Pentonville roads; Nonnie has control of the water and electric companies. There's a roar of laughter when Enid heads off to jail.

Berwyn moves towards the door, 'Alex, Sasha, come - look at the stars; they're brilliant tonight.'

They join him on the doorstep along with Gobaith.

'It should be now, Alex.' Berwyn whispers enigmatically. 'Take Sasha to the orchard quickly, will you? You'll see - I'll watch from here.'

'You okay for a walk under the stars?' Alex asks, turning to Sash and taking her hand.

She squeezes her fingers round his to answer.

They step out into the moonlight, making their way towards the orchard with Gob beside them. Alex is wondering what his uncle meant, he's guessing Berwyn knows something important is about to happen - Berwyn wants them there to see it.

They reach the path, the one they walked earlier, a breeze fans their faces. A cloud covers the moon, but they know the way so keep on going until they reach the mound of earth in the corner and the newly raised slate. The air is cool. It's sweet, rich with late summer scents. They lean into each other, simply taking a moment to be together out there on a warm August night.

Without the moonlight it's dark but Alex can picture the scenery in his mind. In the valley away in the east the River Conwy is flowing towards the sea while above on the far skyline the tall tree tops of Bodnant are standing guard. Away to the west are Tirion Lakes and above them, on the scree slope, stands the blasted fir tree with the high moorland behind it stretching away to the sky.

He speaks gently, 'I haven't read the inscription. Berwyn never encouraged us, did he? Do you think he was embarrassed?'

'Possibly, but I doubt it.'

'Pity the moonlight's gone, I expect he meant we should read the inscription now when he said it should be now - don't you think?'

'I didn't hear what he said,' she breathes her reply. Then adds, 'Oh! I've got this,' taking a pen-like object from her pocket while pressing the button at its head. A beam of light, the size of a pencil, shoots out as they move closer to the slate.

Leaning forward, their heads touching, Alex begins reading the carved words. They're in Welsh. He's not completely fluent but does his best.

Sash shines the light from word to word while Alex's voice rings out stronger as his confidence grows:

'Ci da, ci triw yn troi ei gamre tuag adre,
Y gwaith a'r frwydr hir i gyd ar ben!
Wrth droed fy Meistr, ac afiaith yn fy nghamre
Câf brofi rhyddid o dan ser y nen.

Os peryg ddaw, fe ŵyr y byddaf yno
Yn llamu'r rhedyn ac yn ffroeni'r tir,
I fyny ar y ffridd ger gwal y cadno
Fe âf yn ufudd ar fy sgawtiau hir.

Ond bellach, ffrindiau, 'n fodlon, fe orffw
Yng nghôl fy Meistr mawr, a'i wenau mwyn.
Fe wn y deuwch chithau rhyw ddydd ataf
I brofi 'i gwmni ac i deimlo'i swyn.

Ci da, ci triw yn aros i'ch croesawu,
Y ci a'i ffyddlondeb byth yn pallu.'

He's tingling from head to foot as he finishes, roused by the words.

'What do they mean, Alex?' Sasha whispers, awestruck by his recitation.

Before he can answer there's a swish of movement.

Trotting towards them, just above the ground, is a dapple-grey. The horse is flickering like starlight. On its back is a veiled lady and, as she approaches, they can see all the stages of the moon embroidered in silver on the veil she wears.

Sash notices a sickle moon on the veil over her mouth and a soft, full moon on the veil over her forehead but it is the embroidery of the veil over her eyes that is most striking of all for two half-moons stare straight at her as the lady comes by.

The horse and rider trot right past them. While the lady rides away her black riding cape is flowing behind her and, as it travels, it draws the cloud with it leaving the moon clear so all the landscape behind her is lit in silver light once more. But then she stops, turns to look back at them, the two half moons of her veil alight with sudden brightness. Gracefully, she raises her hand to point at Sash. The next instant a star shoots across the sky, it ends in a flash above Sasha's head … stardust covers her like a fall of snow.

Blinded, Sasha blinks before she can follow the mysterious lady again, riding away once more. As horse and rider climb, the mountains are revealed in the light of the moon. Sash can imagine the lakes, the purple moor she's come to know so well, all silvered over.

'What was that Sash? I think a shooting star crashed to earth just here!' Alex comments excitedly. Then he exclaims, 'Look Sash! There's writing on the other side too. It's neatly chiselled into the slate.'

They step carefully so as not to walk on the mound at its foot. They stand together, hand in hand looking at the words.

'It's in English,' Sasha says and begins to read aloud:

'A good dog, a true dog, running home.
A hard task, a long fight, safely won!
By my Master's side I race and roam;
Through the wild night skies I gladly run.

At scent of danger I will be there.
Bounding above the bracken clad hill
Up on to the moor past the fox's lair
Panting to do my Master's will.

But now dear friends I'm happily gone
To my great Master who smiles on me.
One day I know that you will all come
To join our magnificent company.

A good dog, a true dog waits for you,
A good dog, a true dog, always true.'

There are tears in their eyes as she finishes. All is a blur of silver as they blink.

Sasha's hand is warm in his, a sweet presence.

Unthinkingly, Alex clasps the horn of the whistle with his free hand feeling its hard, smooth grooves. Then he raises it slowly to his lips and blows.

They hear the tinkling music like a swift running stream flowing from the whistle.

'Alex! Look!' Sash gasps.

He follows her outstretched hand. There away to the east are crimson and white colours in the air moving towards them at speed. Behind them is a rider, his horse is dark, difficult to see. As he comes near they see his huge hunting horn, slung over his shoulder and a gold circlet, bright on the top of his hood.

'King Arawn himself!' Alex whispers.

Wonderful crimson eared hounds with dazzling white coats come bounding past, hunting, following a scent - they seem to be following the mysterious lady for they too move swiftly towards the moor.

Close behind them rides their king, the master. His dark cape is green, a rich green.

Sash and Alex watch them into the distance. But when they look back at the mound, they see a gigantic hound standing on top of it! Its coat is a dazzling white, its ears are glowing crimson, round its neck is a plain collar, with a shiny tab. Alex reads out the name, 'Brutus.'

The hound wags its tail on hearing its name.

Then, before Alex or Sash can think, a second hound's there. It's nose to nose with Brutus. Gobaith has grown, he's massive now. He stands tall, his crimson ears erect as he bids farewell to his friend, goodbye to his mentor.

With a single bound, Brutus leaps away to catch Arawn's pack, leaving Gobaith standing beside Alex, watching with ears pricked.

'Look Sash! Can you see Brutus bounding boldly after those others? He must've reached the blasted fir tree already. Oh! Look Sash, I can see the fir tree, it's burning golden like a great beacon!'

Sash's blinking away her tears - yes she can see it too, golden lights away to her right, golden lights on the mountain.

They lean together. Neither speaks. Their heads touch; their cheeks come together.

Alex lets the whistle drop to his chest. He's caressing Sasha's head. Their lips meet. He feels her hand in his back pocket as she pulls him close.

Suddenly, Sasha's laughing. It's a joyful peal, bells ringing in the air, tinkling like a child's triangle, a rainbow of sound like water splashing in a fountain, pure, innocent and so happy. Gob's jumping up. He's placing his paws on both of them, asking to join their embrace. He's a small brown and white spaniel again, refusing to take, 'Down,' for an answer. They begin stroking him, one of his ears still glows red like the sunset while Sasha laughs and laughs.

'Gee bud, now where did I hear a sound as lovely as that?' Jack says to Berwyn as he joins him on the front of the porch.

AFTERWORD

Sasha sniffs. She reaches for yet another tissue…

Her college assignments are due in but she can't raise the energy just now. That bonfire night disco has backfired, leaving her listless in the grip of a cold. Frustrated, she pulls open the bottom drawer of her desk. 'What's that at the back?'

She reaches for the box. It's a cardboard tube, a package that might hold something like a small microscope. For a moment she's confused, 'What's this? Oh! I remember Aled gave it to me! I've gone and forgotten all about it with the start of college. That's awful Sasha.'

Feeling guilty, she takes the lid off. Inside is a roll of papers secured top and bottom by elastic bands. She peels them off, then uses her pencil case and jar of face cream to hold the papers flat on her desk.

"Sasha, here's a piece I've put together. You might find it interesting on a rainy day, haha!

I don't suppose it will assist the Searcher but it should add to your understanding nonetheless. They say knowledge is power. I like to think, 'Understanding brings its own wisdom.' Certainly there's something here for you, writings you need to know. Take care, Aled."

Curious, Sash looks sharply at the script.

… lead us not into …

Temptation

THE TWELVE DAYS OF CHRISTMAS

The Green Knight!

'This most handsome of horsemen drew the eyes of all, especially those of the lady folk present.'

Let me tell you how of all the brave people who ever inhabited Britain, Arthur was the highest in honour - so it's said. Now, this king was at Camelot one Christmastide in the presence of all his loyal lords, members by merit of the Round Table. Their festivities were splendid. They revelled in tournaments, carnivals, jousting, dancing and feasting. Everyone was rejoicing in happiness, their joy was natural as night follows day and dawn grows from dark. In that company were the most lovely ladies ever to be seen, the most famous knights of all time and of course the noblest of all kings.

The year was beginning. New Year gifts were given bountifully, ladies could be heard laughing while their knights looked on. The place was a riot of jollity until the trumpet sounded for food to be served. One thing you should know is Arthur himself wouldn't eat until there had been some bold adventure, a joust risking life against life or something equally daring. He was young, a carefree king, rushing everywhere to the middle of merriment. He wasn't one for sitting down for long but preferred to be on his feet at the side of his friends, so his seat at the table was empty. Imagine his vacant chair at the table, can you?

There was a fanfare of trumpets. The first course was carried forward, shoulder high, mountains of food on massive platters. Silver bowls filled with broth were served, good beer and bright wine flowed. The hub-bub in the hall rose and fell while the lords and ladies feasted.

Unexpectedly into the great hall, from the porch, came an appalling figure.

The drinking ceased. Spoons dropped to plates. Mouths fell open. All the assembly looked on in astonishment. In from the porch he rode. In height he outstripped all men. He was squarely built from his throat to his thigh, sturdy and strong. His limbs were so long that he seemed like he was half a giant. He was exceptionally good looking. Although his back and chest were broad, his haunches were lean. Most certainly he was perfectly proportioned.

His colour was amazing. Somehow, it made his stern face commanding. The huge knight was a brilliant green from head to toe. All his clothes were green! He wore an attractive tunic, tight around the waist and lined with the best fur. The hood lay open on his shoulders. His hair fell in great green tresses over it down his back. Tight, green stockings bulged at his calf, while down near his heels golden spurs were mounted on blocks covered in rich, green silk.

The shin armour he wore was green. The saddle and bridle were green. The massive charger beneath him was green from head to tail. This knight rode without helmet or neck armour, his luxuriant hair curled thick for all to view. It was like ivy around an oak. He carried no shield or spear. In one hand he raised a branch of holly, its red berries like hot coals in a sea of green. In his other hand he held a mighty axe. Its blade shone brightly, looking sharp as a razor, a deadly edge for sure.

His richly embroidered *girdle of bright green could be seen, attached to the shaft of the axe, trimmed with costly tassels.

*(This is a neat detail. The mediaeval writer has written simply, 'A lace lapped aboute … bryzt grene brayden ful riche.' It's a description one barely notices but it's important at the end. Aled)

This strange intruder rode his horse up, down and around the hall, he seemed careless of peril, unworried by danger. He rolled his eyes trying to find the person of highest rank, scanning the assembled knights and ladies, his eyes coming to a stop at Arthur's vacant chair - his horse stamping on the floor, its nostrils flared.

'Who is the commander here?' The rider's powerful question echoed from the sides of the great hall.

All present stared at this knight. Many thought a man of green must be a phantom from Fairyland. They were daunted. A hush like death itself descended on the company.

Not so Arthur, he sensed an adventure. Moving away from his companions, he answered, 'Sir knight, you are welcome. I am king here, King Arthur. Dismount and feast with us.'

'I don't intend to stay in your castle hall. Yet, I heard your knights are the best, the bravest and the most chivalrous. This drew me here. You can see I don't come armed. I have left my spear, my shield, and my helmet at home, riding instead with this branch of holy. I come here in peace and not peril. All I seek is a little sport.'

'If it's a deadly fight you seek, we're for you,' Arthur answered smoothly.

'No, I'm not here for combat. Besides, there's none who could match me amongst these soft faced boys! Look I'm here for a Christmas game, a bit of New Year fun, that's all. Listen, this is what I propose. Let anyone here seize my axe. They may wield it freely to strike one blow at me which I won't resist. The terms of the game are these: whoever dares to strike this blow must come to me in a day and a year to submit to the return blow. It will be my turn then for some harmless fun.' Roaring with laughter, the green challenger looked all around the startled company.

Arthur's knights listened astonished. Not a breath was drawn, not a man moved, all were as if transfixed by death.

The rider twisted in his great saddle. His eyes red like the holly berries, his green brows bent over them in a frown, their bristles glinting while his green beard swung as he turned his head. He looked furious. 'Not so brave after all, not as chivalrous as I had expected.'

Arthur's face flushed as though with shame but his reply was cool, his eye undaunted, 'Your idea of sport is idiotic. No knight here is frightened in the slightest but, if you really insist on this madness, I'm your man.'

Throwing the holly branch to the ground, the rider reached down, seizing Arthur's hand and swung himself out of the saddle. Fiercely he towered over the young king, the axe on his shoulder glinting.

Arthur stretched up, grasped the axe. Slowly at first he began to swing it, whirling it high close to the great, green beard. The stranger stood calmly, he looked as if the king were offering a goblet of drink to toast their friendship.

Before the blow could be dealt, Gawain rushed forward, 'Allow me, my lord!' he cried. 'I'm the weakest here, I'm just a Jack-the-lad, allow me this sport, this act of folly with that fool!'

Arthur brought the axe to the floor. He looked round at the company, heads were nodding, people exclaiming, 'Yes Lord, give it to him! Grant Gawain this quest! Gawain is worthy of this challenge!' Courteously, the king planted the axe beside Gawain, then withdrew, smiling approvingly at the young man's courage.

Gawain grasped the mighty shaft but the stranger stopped him, 'Not so fast young knave, first repeat your name, the terms of the game, then strike.'

'My name is Gawain. After you take this blow from me, I will seek you in a year's time to take your blow. This is my true word.'

'Enough for me, on with the New Year sport, wield the axe, strike me hard,' so saying the green knight swept his locks away from his neck. He was braced for the blow standing with his legs wide apart.

Gawain heaved the great axe into the air. Determined to strike using all his strength, he swung it round, balancing his body. Straining both shoulders and arms he hurled the blade at the smooth neck of the stranger, crunching through bone, slashing through flesh the axe sliced, driving into the floor after the force of the blow, its shaft shivering.

The green head was severed. It fell. It rolled along the ground making people kick it away as the red blood spurted. The strange knight did not fall. He did not even shudder. He strode forward to where his head lay at the foot of a table, picked it up by the hair, turned, took the horse's bridle and sprang up into the saddle. He made some movements, adjusting his riding position, then he turned the head in his hand to face the queen, the lovely Guinevere. It raised its eyelids, alive in his hand, to glare.

Its mouth jerked as it spoke, the sound of its words metallic, robotic on the hushed air: 'Gawain, remember your oath. Ask for "The Knight of Chapelgreen" next New Year. That's the way to find me, to keep your word or forever be called: "Coward!"'

Without another word, the headless rider spurred his horse on out of the hall, his blood spattered head swinging menacingly in his hand.

Arthur was astonished.

Yet he and Gawain laughed loudly at the strange knight. Then Arthur turned to young Guinevere smiling, 'Such cleverness as this suits our Christmastide festivities, suits them marvellously well.'

The massive axe was wrenched out of the floor to be mounted on the wall behind the Round Table. There it remained for all to wonder at, to serve as a reminder to Gawain of the promise he planned to keep.

GAWAIN RIDES OUT

Seasons came and went, time passed. During the All Saints' November feast, Gawain was especially honoured. The end of December approached, with it his day of destiny appeared on the horizon of time present.

The day of departure arrived. Gawain, equipped in his best armour, his knightly gear polished bright as the sun, mounted the gallant horse, Gringolet. Away they galloped in search of the Knight of Chapelgreen. They were gone in a flash.

Far and wide they rode with Gawain continually asking for news of this Green Knight and his Chapelgreen, but to no avail. Riding ever north, the setting sun always away to the left, they passed up through Dyfed and on into *'Norpe Walez …' travelling close to 'Anglesay' then crossing into the 'wyldrenesse of Wyrale'.

*(A few words in their middle English spelling to give a sense of the original : 'North Wales … Anglesey …wilderness of the Wirral….' Aled.)

At this time the wilderness of the Wirral was a den of robbers, an abode of wanted men, a truly dangerous place. Added to this was the extreme winter weather, icy cold nights followed by days of sleet, hail and snow.

Then on Christmas Eve, Gringolet entered a wild, wooded valley. Frosted tree branches, heavy with ice, hung above the way; a few brave birds piped some thin music as knight and horse passed below. Deep within the wood, high to his right, Gawain saw the round towers of a grand castle, looming ever higher above them as he rode.

Gawain called out loudly to the keeper of the castle, 'I need a place to stay this Christmas Day!'

Right courtly hospitality was shown to Gawain, while Gringolet was stabled in luxury. The weary horse was given a floor covered in clean, dry straw, a manger of hay, baskets of dry oats - cool troughs of fresh mountain water.

The lord of the castle was a mighty man. He was very tall, strong as granite, a huge figure. His red beard flamed out from his chin. He was bright, friendly, quickly making his visitor feel at ease.

Gawain was given: apartments of the best, a page to attend to his every need, an invitation into the lord's family for Christmastide.

Soon he sat before a charcoal fire to feast on soups, fish of every kind, while he drank many a goblet of wine with his host. It was not long before they discovered their guest came from Arthur's renowned court, a Round Table knight, Sir Gawain. They were honoured to receive such a guest, counting his visit as a special Christmas gift.

THE LOVELY LADY

Gawain couldn't help noticing the fairness of the lady of the castle. Her body, her complexion, her whole manner made her the most beautiful lady he had ever seen, even excelling Guinevere. Her presence made his Christmas stay with the generous lord of the castle all the more delightful.

After Christmas, Gawain said he must now leave to keep his promise.

'What promise is this?' asked his host, wanting to keep Gawain with them for all twelve days of festivities.

Gawain told him of his quest. How in four days' time he must meet the Green Knight at the Chapelgreen to receive his blow and keep his word. He explained how he'd no idea where this Chapelgreen was so must leave immediately.

'Ah!' his host exclaimed. 'Now I know why you made the perilous journey from Arthur's kingdom and in winter too! But worry not, I happen to know the whereabouts of this Green Chapel. It's only a morning's ride from here. So you can stay on with us for the next three days and still arrive in time to keep faith with this Green Knight.'

Feelings of friendship for his great host doubled in Gawain's heart at this happy turn. He knew he could keep his tryst, his journey was at an end and now he could enjoy the remaining days of Christmas in the company of his new friends.

Before he could speak the host exclaimed, 'The winter trek has tired you out! Yet you feasted with us hardly sleeping. Gawain, my friend, you must rest before greeting the Green Knight. Stay here until New Year. Lie in, take your ease, eat, you must rest, gain your strength, before your great test. My wife shall keep you company while I rise at dawn to hunt all day.'

It was an attractive proposition. Gawain was not slow to agree to it.

'One thing more,' said the lord of the castle, 'let's make an arrangement. Whatever I catch out hunting, I'll give to you provided you give me anything you get while resting here.'

With a clasp of arms, a slap on the shoulders, the two friends agreed.

The following morning, the lord of the castle went hunting at dawn while Gawain slept late in his curtained bed. As Gawain snoozed, a suspicious sound entered his consciousness. The door of his bedchamber was being stealthily opened. He took up a corner of the curtain drawn around his bed to look unseen at the incomer.

It was the lady of the castle, the loveliest of women, who secretly closed the door. Embarrassed, Gawain lay flat, pretending to sleep.

Silently she picked up the curtain, slipped in and softly sat on the side of his bed. She kept watch over him, waiting for him to wake.

Gawain lay there wondering what to make of this marvel!

He thought he should perhaps find out what she wanted by asking her. So he pretended to be just waking ... stirring ... stretching ... showing the greatest surprise on seeing this beauty seated above him.

She looked down on him, her rosy lips, her lovely chin, her fair cheek. She took his breath away. Laughing in a loving way she teased, 'Hello Sir Gawain, you do sleep insecurely! I must say, it was easy to slip in here to capture you. Now you can make what treaty you like but I'm going to tie you to your bed for sure.'

'Good day, wonderful lady,' Gawain answered happily like one in a dream, 'you may do with your prisoner what you wish for I surrender completely. All I can do is to beg for your favour, dear lady.'

'Perhaps I will take pity on you, what do you crave?'

'Allow me to rise and dress. Then we can enjoy some sweet conversation.'

'Not granted. I have a better plan. I'm going to hold you down in your bed on both sides, my chevalier. Now that I have caught you in my chains I'm going to keep you here. I know I've captured the renowned Sir Gawain himself, a knight ladies hold in the highest regard because of his courtesy. Since I've got the one everybody fancies, I'm going to take my time with him, enjoying him completely.' Laughing softly, she bent her face close to his, adding in little more than a whisper, 'So you may do what you like with my youthful body, Sir Gawain, I'm ready to serve you as you desire.'

'In truth I'm the luckiest man alive, fair lady! Although I'm not the hero you think I am, it would give me pure joy to render you any service in speech, thought or action. I am ever ready to give pleasure to you, surely the most perfect lady living today.'

'There are many ladies, noble knight, who would love to have you to hold under their hands like I'm doing here.'

'Dear lady, I can tell now you're someone with a free, a most generous nature, but I don't feel worthy of your praise.'

'Sir Gawain, if I were choosing a husband you'd be my choice, you're so handsome, humble - a most noble knight for sure,' she answered smiling, the tip of her tongue showing between her teeth.

'You chose a better lord, fair lady.'

They talked together, lingering, she adoringly, Gawain held there by courtesy, of course, but also by an unspoken longing that kept him under her spell.

When the time came for her to go, the lady said, 'People will say it couldn't have been the real Sir Gawain!'

'What do you mean, fair lady?'

'No-one would believe the noble Gawain would've spent so long in a lady's company as you have - without requesting a kiss in courtesy,' she answered archly, twirling a lock of her hair with her finger.

'I beg a kiss, fair one, if it doesn't offend you,' Gawain responded.

She leaned over, caught him in her arms and kissed him lovingly once.

At nightfall the lord of the castle returned. He brought with him venison and deerskin all of which he presented to Gawain as they had agreed. Gawain praised this lord for the thriving huntsman he evidently was saying, 'Such wonderful game from winter hunting I haven't seen in the last seven years! In return, I must give you what I won here as I rested idly.' Then he put his arms around the lord's neck, hugging him lovingly, and kissed him sweetly, 'Here's what I gained today.'

'Thank you, Gawain, that's good but it'd be better still if you'd whisper gently in my ear how you came by this sweet kiss.'

'That's not a part of our agreement, my friend, so I'll keep my own counsel,' Gawain answered, discreetly.

The following morning the lord of the castle set off again at dawn for a day's hunting. This time they found and pursued the greatest wild-boar that had ever roamed the forest. It took them from morning to noon and from noon to dusk to defeat the noble beast but as night fell the lord returned to his castle bearing this magnificent boar to present to Gawain.

Meanwhile, Gawain rested. As the sun rose the lady of the castle entered his bedchamber. She sidled sweetly into the room, slipped under his bed curtains and sat once more beside him. Gawain made this beautiful visitor welcome, showing her every courtesy.

After some time the lovely lady exclaimed, 'I can hardly believe you are Sir Gawain, he surely would have paid more attention to what he learnt yesterday and would have acted by now?'

'I don't know what you mean, fair one, how am I at fault?'

'I invited your kiss yesterday, didn't I? So you should have taken a kiss this morning, surely? Especially as no-one could refuse you anyway.'

'Oh, but you might have refused me, then I would have been in the wrong,' Gawain explained.

'You're so strong, Gawain, you could take what you want from a defenceless person like me, you could do as you like with me, couldn't you?'

'Using strength against a fair lady is not my way, dear one,' Gawain answered, 'but if you would like to give me a kiss, you're most welcome.'

The beautiful hostess bent over to kiss him softly on his forehead. The lovely lady stayed on his bed a long time, talking, laughing, enticing him with her feminine charms. Eventually, she leant over to kiss him again and left.

In the evening the lord of the castle exchanged what he'd won with Gawain. He presented him with the magnificent wild-boar he'd caught hunting. Then Gawain clasped his arms around his host to kiss him softly not once but twice.

The lord of the castle laughed loudly, 'I can see you're beating me easily at this game, Sir Gawain!' he exclaimed in good humour. 'Now be a good sport, go on, tell me how you came by such favours.'
Gawain laughed. 'You know my lord, that's not part of our agreement.'

It was New Year's Eve. The castle hall was a place of mirth. The lady of the castle was Gawain's constant companion, she flirted with him bewitchingly. The true knight was discomposed in the presence of so many, including her husband, to be so prettily beset but he dealt with her politely without bringing disgrace upon them, receiving her amorous advances with courtesy.

When New Year's Day broke, the lord of the castle was already in his saddle and off hunting, while Gawain lay dreaming in his curtained bed. The lady of the castle tiptoed quickly into Gawain's room as the sun rose. Her robe was ravishing, of costly fur, but so open her back and breasts were bare. She threw open the window saying, 'How can you sleep so deeply, Gawain?' Before the waking knight could speak, she crossed the room, slipped through his bed curtains and kissed him sweetly.

As Gawain looked on her beauty, he flushed with passion. She bent over him so lovingly he felt he must either allow her embraces wherever they might lead or rudely push her away. Yet he remembered the lord of the castle's generosity. 'This can never happen,' he thought to himself. So he used laughter to deflect her advances.

Now she pouted. 'I swear there is some beautiful maiden who's won your love already!' she exclaimed.

Ever truthful, Gawain replied, 'No fair lady, I have no such love but am free, single.'

'That's a disappointing answer,' she sighed, 'I'll kiss you once and go then,' so saying she bent over him and kissed him softly. 'Yet before I go from here, give me a keepsake. Something I can remember these sweet mornings by.'

'I'm on a strange errand, fair lady. I travel with no treasures. There's nothing appropriate I can offer you, forgive me.'

She pouted. Beautiful she looked as she stood a moment in thought. 'Even though you can give me nothing, Sir Gawain, let me give you this precious ring, my parting gift.'

'Dear lady. As I can't give anything to you, I'll accept nothing,' Gawain said with a smile.

'I see my ring is too valuable. Yet you'll not reject this green girdle I'm wearing around my waist,' the lady answered, removing her sash with a flourish. Its cloth was shimmering green, a varying green with different shades coming and going. It had a golden hem but was otherwise plain except for an embroidered raven on its edge.

Gawain could see its beauty. He knew he would please her by accepting it but as he was going to his death the very next day he refused it saying, 'I'll touch no treasure at all, dear lady.'

'So,' she said breathlessly, 'you're refusing even this simple keepsake? You think it's worthless, I suppose? Yet there's something really special in its weave, I promise. Listen, the man who binds this round his body, next to his flesh, is safe from all attacks. While he's wearing this girdle he cannot be killed by any blow or assailant.'

Gawain looked at the girdle with keener interest. He saw it would be a good plan to wear this special garment during his meeting with the Green Knight, the very next day. It would be a likely means of escaping certain death. So he allowed her to persuade him into taking it.

Smiling slyly, she handed the girdle over, begging him to conceal this 'New Year's gift' from her husband for her sake, asking him to always keep it secret.

He promised her he would.

Pleased with his promise, knowing him to be a man of his word, a true knight, she took his face in her hands, giving him the sweetest of kisses, a kiss so soft it melted his heart as she allowed her lips to linger. Then she skipped lightly across the bedroom and left, gently pulling the door closed behind her.

All this time and more, the lord of the castle hunted a brave fox. It led his hounds round and about through wood and dale. Eventually, the outnumbered creature was caught and killed, the poor thing was skinned. Dusk was falling when the lord returned to his castle with a fox skin to present to Gawain.

Gawain was rested and in high spirits after his three days of relaxation. When he saw the lord of the castle he embraced him saying, 'Here are my day's takings,' I give them freely. He then kissed his friend softly three times on the face.

'You've won precious things indeed!' exclaimed his host. 'My offering's a poor one in comparison, here take this wretched fox skin. That's all I won today.'

As they parted on that last evening of Gawain's stay, the knight said, 'Don't forget your promise of guiding me to the Chapelgreen in the morning,' giving his host a reminder.

'Have no fear, everything I promised I shall perform.'

THE BLOW

The following morning, dressed in his knightly gear, with the lady's green girdle carefully wrapped, out of sight but tight around his body, Gawain set forth mounted on Gringolet. His host had provided a trusty guide to take him to the appointed place where he would meet the Green Knight to keep his oath.

The weather, on this second day of January, had turned. Bitter winds bringing ice and snow whistled in from the north, filling the dales with rich drifts of snow. The guide and the knight rode out into the high country, past crags where the cold clung, across moors shrouded in freezing fog, along heights where hats of icy clouds hid the mountaintops.

As the appointed hour approached, the guide stopped at a great cliff, from where the snow stretched on all sides. 'I have guided you faithfully, Sir Gawain. Now, you are very close to Chapelgreen. Like many in our castle I've grown to admire you during your stay with us. You're a man of your word, valiant and true. But listen to me, in the wilderness yonder dwells the worst enemy on earth. Avoid him if you can, he's deadly. He's bigger than four men, a killing machine. You'd be wise to turn your horse in another direction. Go anywhere but there!' he exclaimed, pointing down a rugged ravine directly below.

'You mean well, friend, but I have given my word,' came

the resolute answer.

'God save you then! I dare venture no further! Adieu!' Away the guide went, back along the way they had travelled.

Gawain urged Gringolet forward. Slowly they edged down the slippery ground, twisting round huge boulders white with snow, Gringolet, his head close to the floor making the descent, step by careful step. Eventually they came into the valley. Here a stream flowed, bubbling brown, racing along.

Now Gawain came to the strangest chapel he had ever seen. It was a hollowed out mound, a gaping crag, a burial barrow covered in lichen and moss. A devilish place, at best it was a fairy den.

He dismounted, hooked Gringolet's reins on a tree branch, and entered. It had an opening at each end, the air within was dank. He could tell it was a cheerless dwelling. Gawain was just wondering if his meeting was with the evil one himself, who'd disguised himself in green, when his attention was drawn by a noise outside.

He turned to listen. From the rocks, up above the brook came a barbaric sound. Screeching from side to side in that hidden valley, echoed the sound of metal on stone! It wailed like water in a millrace, it clamoured like the shriek of women, it clattered over the stones like the falling head of a helmeted knight.

'No doubt this fearful din, the sharpening of a great blade, is to welcome me here,' Gawain thought to himself.

Then he stepped out of the barrow shouting loudly, 'I'm here as I promised! I, the knight, Sir Gawain, have arrived for our game! Come at once to take your turn, act now or lose your chance!'

A sudden silence fell on the dale.

Gawain waited in the cold air, his eyes on the slopes above the stream.

'Wait there!' shouted one hidden close by above him.

Moments later the green figure emerged from a cave. In his hands he carried a huge battle-axe, its sharpened blade gleaming with menace. The Green Knight strode over the ground in easy bounds but when he came to the brook he plunged the shaft of his axe into the rushing water, using it like a pole to vault across, keeping his feet dry.

Foot sure on the wet snow, the Green Knight strode over to Gawain, 'Welcome to my dwelling Sir Gawain, I see you kept your word. It's what I expected, of course. Now I shall pay you back for the blow you gave me a year ago.'

'I'm ready for you,' Gawain replied, 'you may strike your best blow now, but mind: you'll take one blow only.'

At that the Green Knight bellowed in laughter, his green beard shaking with mirth, 'Take off your helmet then I'll only need a single swipe.'

Gawain stood - his bare neck ready to receive the blow about to fall.

The assailant raised his axe high, whirling it to inflict a mighty blow then swung it down savagely.

Gawain flinched as his glance caught the falling blade.

So the Green Knight heaved the axe head up out of its strike. 'What's this?' he roared. 'Did I not stand still when you took your blow? Does your flinching show me to be the braver knight?'

'I'll not flinch again so get on with it.'

His assailant seemed mad with anger, his temper roused. Once again he raised the huge weapon swinging it savagely, swishing it through the air towards Gawain's bare neck. Gawain braced himself for the death blow.

However, the Green Knight brought the blade up suddenly. 'Just checking you weren't going to flinch again,' he growled at Gawain.

Now it was Gawain's turn for anger, 'I think you're scared of your own shadow. Every second you waste brings you closer to losing your chance of returning my bold blow of yesteryear.'

'Right this is it then!' roared his opponent. Down the mighty axe fell, parting Gawain's flesh so that his blood spurted onto the snow. It was only a nick, a flesh wound.

Gawain skipped away shouting, 'Cease your blows! I've received blow for blow without resisting just as we agreed!'

'Have no fear, brave knight, I'll keep my word,' came the swift response.

'So we're quits then!' Gawain exclaimed.

His opponent gave him a searching look, 'Understand this Gawain. The first pretend blow was for your first night when you kept our bargain, giving me my wife's fair kiss. The second fake blow was for your second night when you again played fair, giving me my wife's sweet kisses. The nick you received on the third blow is for the green girdle you're wearing which belongs to me.'

Gawain blanched, then blushed with shame.

The waters of the brook gurgled past the two knights.

Suddenly, Gawain undid the silken knot shoving the girdle into his opponent's hand, 'Here take it, I'm no better than a thief! It's rightfully yours.'

The Green Knight laughed, 'That's true, but since you admit it and have taken your punishment from the blade of my axe you're forgiven. It wasn't greed that tempted you, or lust, but the love of your own life. So I'm giving you the girdle as a sign of our friendship. Keep it safe, it's yours now,' he said, handing the girdle to Gawain.

'I'll wear it as a sign of my weakness,' Gawain answered, smiling sadly before adding, 'it'll keep me humble my friend.' He tied the shimmering lace around his neck, unhooked Gringolet, riding out of the dale, a wiser knight.

◆ ◆ ◆

"Sasha, the above's very much my own translation. You may like to consult the original. I can recommend a recent edition, 'Sir Gawain and the Green Knight,' Norman Davis, published by the OUP 1967 based on an earlier work edited by Tolkein and Gordon. You may find the northern Middle English difficult at first but it's worth persevering.

Now turn the page to take a look at the next tale, it's from 'The Mabinogion.' It'll intrigue you. Aled."

PWYLL PRINCE OF DYFED

One day, the renowned prince, the friend of King Arthur, Pwyll Prince of Dyfed didn't live up to his name. He failed in wisdom, acted without sound judgement, giving into temptation. Here's what happened.

Pwyll was alone in the forest. He was hunting his pack of hounds but had lost them in the eagerness of the hunt. He reined in his horse blowing his hunting horn. He listened expectantly. Surely he would soon catch the baying of his hounds carried on the wind? He knew their cry so well he'd easily pick it up even if they were miles away. To his surprise he heard a very unusual hunting pack coming his way, it approached fast, the unearthly baying sounding ever louder in his ears. Then a magnificent stag burst into the clearing in front of him. Its coat was as white as the moon. Moments later the place was filled with hounds. It was an eerie sight. The hounds gleamed brilliant white with red markings which glowed like burning coals at their ears. The stag was caught and brought quickly to ground.

Pwyll was suddenly tempted. 'I could drive these otherworld hounds off, then call my hungry pack to feed them on this dead stag. There's no-one to see me do it, besides these ethereal hounds don't need earthly food but my pack does,' he reasoned.

He rode forward fiercely. The weird hounds bounded off so he called his dogs blowing loudly, urgently, on his hunting horn. They bounded to his side and he feasted his whole pack on the white stag.

While his dogs were still eating, a rider approached - a hunting horn slung around his neck. His riding cloak was the colour of mist, he looked majestic on his dapple-grey stallion as he rode, surrounded by the strange pack. 'I know who you are but I won't give you the time of day!' the rider in grey shouted.

'Why's that?' Pwyll inquired.

'It's because you have the manners of a lout, that's why,' came the stern answer.

'What loutish behaviour do you mean?' Pwyll asked, blushing.

'You know very well. You have just driven away the pack that killed the stag before they could eat what was theirs so that you could feed your own dogs. Do you deny it?' he asked angrily, looking at Pwyll's hounds. 'I'll not bother to take revenge on you. You can feel your shame yourself. It does you more harm than the loss of a hundred stags.'

Pwyll hung his head. He was mortified. 'You're right sire, I'm in the wrong here. The stag my dogs have just eaten wasn't theirs to eat nor mine to give them. I see I have lost your respect. Tell me how I can right this wrong and gain your friendship.'

'Admitting you're in the wrong is a good start. You should know that I'm King Arawn. My kingdom is in the Inside or

Other World.'

'You should know I'm Pwyll, Prince of Dyfed, this forest here is in my kingdom.'

'I know who you are,' King Arawn answered. 'Now, I'll tell you how you can redeem yourself and gain my friendship, since that's what you wish.'

'I do.'

'I have a neighbour who is always attacking me. He is an Other World king, his name is Hafgan. You could help me easily to rid my kingdom of his oppression, would you be willing to do that?'

'Yes.'

'Right then, I'm going to make a firm friend of you, Pwyll. Here's my plan. You and I will change places. You'll take my body shape and live as me, ruling my Inside or Other World kingdom. I will give you the most beautiful woman to share your life and sleep in your bed. No-one in my kingdom will realise you're not me because the disguise will be perfect.'

'But how am I going to find this enemy of yours to keep my promise to you?'

'Don't worry about that a meeting has been arranged already for a year from tonight. We're to meet where the ford crosses the stream. Let me warn you to only give Hafgan one blow. One blow is all that's needed so on no account strike him more than once.'

'What will happen in Dyfed while I'm gone?'

'I'm going to rule as if I'm you. My disguise will be so

perfect no-one will realise it isn't you Pwyll. Come with me now if you still agree to our friendship, I'll lead you all the way to my kingdom,' Arawn said, taking hold of Pwyll's outstretched hand to give it a firm shake.

They rode together through the forest, their two packs mingling freely so that each earthly hound had an ethereal shadow beside it. When they reached the edge of his kingdom, Arawn stopped. He directed Pwyll to ride through a dark avenue where yew trees grew densely on both sides of the bridle path as it passed a mighty waterfall. 'Ride on alone now, rule my people well this next year, as I know you will my friend.' So saying, he turned his horse's head back towards Dyfed and rode off in the twilight, his shining hounds lighting the path as he travelled.

Now Pwyll entered Arawn's kingdom. He rode into the court. The hall and rooms were richly adorned. Two boys ran out to remove his boots, a groom led his horse away, and two knights came to change his hunting clothes and to robe him in silk and gold.

Pwyll spent the year feasting, singing and leading the hunt. Beside him in the court, his constant smiling companion, was the Queen. She was the most beautiful woman he had ever seen, he loved her friendly disposition and easy chatter. She was gracious, noble, the loveliest companion any man could wish to have. Everyone could see how much they loved each other, how tender and close they were. Each evening they went early to bed, closed the bedroom door, and shared the large, curtained bed, sleeping and dreaming as lovers do.

When the appointed day came, the Queen was seated in

her place, beautiful as ever, but her lovely cheek was pale like a white rose. 'Today, you must go to the ford, my lord, be careful.'

'Dearest lady, there's nothing to fear,' Pwyll reassured her.

With a few chosen knights, Pwyll rode to the banks of the stream. It was the coldest time of year. The great yew trees were heavy with snow, the rushing water of the river was a sparkling band in the white landscape. Pwyll rode along the snow covered bank, looking up while he rode for Arawn's enemy. All he saw was snow, trees, rocks and the racing water.

Then he heard the jingling of bells coming from the wood on the far bank. Louder and louder the bridle harness jingled as the great king approached, then he suddenly appeared riding out from the green wood in a shower of snow, Hafgan the Mighty. 'I see you have kept the appointment we made, Arawn!' he bellowed across the water.

Before answer was made, one of Arawn's knights rode forward. His words rang out for all to hear: 'This combat is between our two kings alone! This single combat will decide who rules all this land! We must observe but may not interfere!'

The kings now charged, coming together in the middle of the river at the ford. Pwyll's lance struck Hafgan's shield so violently the shield shattered. The blow knocked Hafgan out of his saddle sending him flying through the air, crashing back to the bank he'd ridden down when making his attack.

Hafgan knew he'd received a fatal blow. 'Lord, I was never

planning to take your land so you really had no right to kill me!' he cried. 'Since you have given me my death blow, I urge you to show me mercy by killing me quickly.'

Pwyll remembered Arawn's warning that he should only strike a single blow. 'No,' he answered, 'find someone else to do it. I am not willing to kill you as you lie there on the ground.'

Then Hafgan urged his nobles to carry him off to die.

All the nobles present acknowledged that Pwyll, whom they thought was Arawn, was the only king of the Other World Kingdom. By noon of the next day the two kingdoms had become one and were under his control.

It was the end of the year so Pwyll rode away to meet up with Arawn as agreed. The two friends were very pleased to see each other. Arawn gave Pwyll back his proper form so that he was once again Prince of Dyfed and took back his own so that he was King of the Other World Kingdom once more. Then they rode back to their own countries.

When Pwyll arrived in his realm he began to question his noblemen about his rule during the last year. He heard nothing but good ... never before have you ruled so wisely ... never have you been so kind a ruler as you have been this last year ... never have you been so generous to others with your goods, actions and words as in this year which has just passed!

Arawn returned to his court and was most happy to see his nobles but they made little fuss of him for he was no different than the Arawn they had seen every day. He spent the day happily conversing with his wife, he'd missed her company especially during the last year. He retired to bed with her when the time came, and began indulging in talk, love play and affection.

She soon put a stop to that, 'Why this change tonight?' she asked. 'Why is your attitude so different tonight to what it has been all this last year?'

She turned her back on him.

He spoke to her a second time lovingly.

Still she did not respond.

He tried again indulging in some gentle affection a third time.

She remained unmoved.

'What have I done? Why won't you speak to me?' he asked.

'Well, surely you know how for the whole of this last year you've never so much as said a word to me in the privacy of our own bed?' she answered.

'What? Surely, we've always talked together here in our own bed, my dearest one?'

'All I know is this last year as soon as you've come to bed you've turned from me, wrapped the bedclothes around you and spoken not one word. You haven't even turned your face towards me let alone anything more.'

Arawn lay in bed thinking of the integrity of his friend, Pwyll. He knew now Pwyll was a true prince, loyal, steadfast and trustworthy. The error with the stag was atoned for, completely erased by the keeping of their agreement so completely, so honestly.

Eventually, he exclaimed, 'Don't blame me, I've not slept or lain with you for the last year!'

After she'd heard the whole story his wife smiled and said, 'A noble lord indeed to fight off the temptations of the flesh here in our bed whilst keeping his promise to you!'

NAUGHTY SASHA

"Sasha, there's a lot of common ground in these two stories written at about the same period in different realms but geographically not so far apart either. I hope you've found them thought provoking.

Temptation at its heart is always a fraud, a cheat. When we give in to temptation we know it won't give us the satisfaction it seems to offer, yet we humans seem prone to it in one form or another, don't you agree? Once we're tempted we're almost caught.

It's the case with Gawain and Pwyll who are two of the best. They are brave, true and able to resist the temptations of the flesh yet both fail as well as triumph.

I expect you know all about Pwyll by now and his romantic attachment to the mysterious horsewoman, the lovely Rhiannon, magical stuff. I've only selected the parts of his myth that align with the Gawain legend since I know you already have the rest of it anyway.

Yours as ever, Aled."

Yes. Sash had read the legend. She'd found Rhiannon, the beautiful rider whom no-one could catch, quite fascinating. She'd especially liked Rhiannon's attitude. The way she'd evaded her arranged marriage choosing Pwyll instead, managing everything herself and calling Pwyll a fool to his face when he'd been too generous with his promises - the stupid man!

Reaching for another tissue, Sash rolls up the papers, secures them with the rubber bands and pops them back in their holder. 'Lots to think about there ... I must write to Aled before Christmas,' she thinks to herself.

Deciding to put the tube away in her cupboard for now, she crosses the room and pushes it to the back but sneezes suddenly, making it jerk, dislodging Sal's diary which falls on the floor at her feet.

'Clumsy me,' she thinks. Her neck's stiff, aching with the cold.

She scoops the booklet up but instead of replacing it in the nook she's made specially at the front, she takes her sister's diary to her desk and flicks it open.

The first words she sees are pure Sal:

Private!!! You shouldn't be reading this without permission!!!

They bring tears. She reaches for a tissue to stop them splashing onto Sal's precious diary.

Soon she's lost in Sal's world. She feels her way along the smooth alabaster floor of the palace, looking up at the golden haze. It's so thick she cannot see the ceiling of the long corridor but she can hear the trumpeters begin their marching music as she passes each doorway along the way.

Once she's reached the far end, she sees the dragon appear beside the black door, her mouth's open as she watches the green and red letters spell out, *Cymru, West Window.*

The door swings in on itself and she enters. Evocative smells bring back memories of her Cornish holiday and Bodmin Moor. She hears a curlew call. Under her feet the rough, wooden floor feels warm.

Light is flooding the room from the window. It's blinding her. She shuts her eyes against it. The blood-red of her eyelids fill with stars, golden stars. Stars that are different - not the silver of icy stars she's seen on a winter night - but warm like the sun!

Turning to her right, shielding her eyes from the light, she opens them to see a tapestry. It's magnificent. She traces the woven figures with her eyes: suns, moons, stars and white deer, created thread by thread by a seamstress of immense skill. Strange craft or art indeed for as she looks red thread shouts from a green background, stitching out the words:

Be Fearless and Brave but Forgiving too

Green thread then covers up the words, shimmering different shades, various colours but always green until every bit is green, before red stitching returns to cry out:

The Hound of Arawn comes
He runs

Now the green tide is back washing over the letters. Then the red message returns, boldly exhorting her, word by word :

Be brave
Be fearless
Be free

Her mind fills with bees busy in the sunshine about their hive, before the green flows in to envelop everything. Back comes the red, confident in its message:

Always recall
Forgiveness is
The balm of all

Aenlic Angharad

She's expecting the whole tapestry to turn completely green once more but is surprised to see a raven appear underneath the name. It is black. It gleams like wet coal, and looks at her with a green eye! Beside it appears the name *Bran*, in red stitching.

She gives a cry of recognition, 'Bran!'

A wave of tiredness pulls her down, coming from nowhere. She has to rest. She leans forward onto the desk, closing her eyes … allowing the snooze to come.

When she wakes, the room seems colder. It is like a freezer. For a moment she doesn't know where she is but then sees Sal's diary open on the desk in front of her and remembers. She's still hungover from her snooze and this yucky cold - it's making her shudder. She flicks a coil of hair away from her eye then slides her fingers through her fringe smoothing it down. It needs a trim. She tries a deep breath, inhaling slowly through her blocked nose, lowering her diaphragm, deliberately drawing the air up through the nostrils hearing it hiss as it comes crawling along her sore sinuses.

Looking at the diary she reads Sal's message:

Only to be read during the twelve days of Christmas. Or else!

The pages are held together by a clump of small paper clips but one of them has become dislodged. Knowing she'd better put it back she picks it up, small and cold between her finger and thumb it's a bit slippery.

She grabs the edge of the pages to slide it into place but clumsily knocks the other clips away instead, dropping the clip she's holding, so that the page begins to unfurl. She covers it over with her hand, looking away as she does so.

Perhaps she should read it? Sal wouldn't mind, surely she wouldn't? After all, we're going to be in Cornwall for Christmas. Wouldn't it be best to know this bit now, before we go? Perhaps it will mean a change of plan or mention something we're going to need? Reluctant to go against her sister's instructions she resists, but she's longing to know what's there.

It's just Sal being silly, she didn't really mean it. It's just a game. Well, she wouldn't mind, whatever.

Going against Sal's wishes she looks down at the uncovered page, her curiosity, her confidence in her closeness to Sal, her ability to persuade Sal to let her, all combine to override her sense of guilt.

There's no writing on the page. It's white as snow, empty. She will have to turn it over to see what's next.

Sash sneezes. She needs another tissue. She's freezing cold. 'Why's she so cold?' Her teeth are chattering. They unnerve her. 'Something isn't right!'

'What's she doing?'

Wrong ... wrong ... wrong!

She looks in horror at the pile of paper clips. Did she violate Sal's wish, her dead sister's wish? It's been written plainly enough. She knows she did. For a moment she did look to read what was there but was saved by her sneezing and because nothing was written on the first page!

Disappointment shivers on the air.

She hasn't read it. She's not going to read it now! She'll wait until the right time.

She begins to seal the pages with the clips just as Sal herself did. There's a click at the door, the sound of the lock sliding into place as if someone has just left. It's a sound she barely notices as she's busy with the diary.

Her face is flushed, warm with embarrassment. 'Sorry Sal,' she breathes, 'I don't know what I was thinking!'

She crosses to her cupboard.

Placing the diary back in its special nook, 'Sorry Sal,' she repeats. Then adds pulling the door closed, 'Naughty Sash, naughty, naughty Sasha.'

She knows really it must just be her imagination, but surely she can hear Sal's laughter, showering from above, rinsing her ears, cleansing her fault? Yes, it's that joyous giggle of hers. Listen, she's calling softly, 'Until the twelve days of Christmas then, Sash-a!'

BIBLIOGRAPHY

J.A.W. Bennett and G.V. Smithers, *Early Middle English Verse and Prose*
(Oxford at the Clarendon Press 1968, Second Edition)

Bryan Johnathan, *Eye Can Write - A Memoir of a Child's Silent Soul Emerging*
(LAGOM 2018)

Davies Sioned, *The Mabinogion*
(Oxford University Press 2007)

Davis Norman, *Sir Gawain and the Green Knight*
Edited by J.R.R. Tolkein and E.V. Gordon
(Oxford University Press 1967)

Gantz Jeffrey, *The Mabinogion*
(Penguin 1976)

Stone Brian, *Sir Gawain and the Green Knight*
(Penguin 1959)

Whitelock Dorothy, *Sweet's Anglo-Saxon Reader in Prose and Verse*
(Oxford University Press 1967)

Printed in Dunstable, United Kingdom

68020994R00127